The Vanishing Point

By: Bushra Hafeez

Copyright © 2024 Bushra Hafeez

All rights reserved.

No part of this book may be used or reproduced, distributed, or transmitted in any form or by any means, including photocopying, recording, or other electronic or mechanical methods, without the proper written permission of the publisher, except in the case of brief quotations apart, embodied in critical reviews and certain other non-commercial uses permitted by copyright law. Use of this publication is permitted solely for personal use and must include full attribution of the material's source.

Paperback ISBN: 9798334972445

Contents

Prologue   7

Chapter 1
The Warning   10

Chapter 2
Silent Unseen Connections   26

Chapter 3
A Promise And A Proposal   48

Chapter 4
Clues In The Dark   57

Chapter 5
The Waterside Revelation   75

Chapter 6
Confronting Hill   96

Chapter 7
Veil Of Secrets   113

Chapter 8
The Handwriting Of Betrayal   139

Chapter 9
Clara's Revelation   147

Chapter 10
The Dark Truth Unveiled 156

Chapter 11
A New Dawn 171

Epilogue 179

About The Author 183

Note From The Author 184

For God and my Parents, Hafeez and Fatima.

Thank you for everything.

"She was unstoppable, not because she did not have failures or doubts, but because she continued on despite them."

—Beau Taplin

Prologue

Five years ago,

That day, Clara's behavior was anything but ordinary. She moved through the Harvest Festival preparations like a ghost, her usually bright eyes clouded with a distant, haunted look. Typically, this was her favorite event, one she embraced with infectious enthusiasm. But today, she seemed on edge, her gaze flickering to her watch every few minutes as if counting down to something—or someone.

As the sun dipped below the horizon, casting long shadows across Silver Creek, the festival came alive. The air buzzed with laughter, music, and the scent of freshly baked pies. I was stationed at the book sale table, doing my best to keep up with the steady stream of festival-goers.

Customers came and went, but my mind kept drifting to Clara.

"Clara?" I called out, my voice barely audible over the clamor of the festival. Moments earlier, I had seen her slip away from the table, her figure disappearing into the growing darkness near the old oak tree by the creek. My heart pounded with a mixture of fear and confusion as I followed her.

The shadows deepened as I neared the tree. Clara stood there, her back to me, staring into the distance. "Clara, what's going on?" I asked, my voice trembling.

She turned slowly, her face pale and her eyes wide with something I couldn't quite decipher. "I'll be right back," she whispered, her voice nearly lost in the rustling leaves.

Before I could respond, she disappeared into the darkness. Panic surged through me as I searched frantically, calling out her name. The joyous sounds of the festival now felt cruelly out of place, a stark contrast to the terror building within me.

"Clara!" I shouted, my voice breaking. There was no response, only the eerie rustling of leaves and the distant strains of music. With each passing minute, my fear grew, turning my search into a desperate chase.

She was gone and vanished without a trace.

The festival's echoes faded, replaced by an unsettling silence. The cheerful lights seemed dimmer, and the music sounded hauntingly distant. My heart felt heavy, burdened by the uncertainty of what lay ahead. Clara had vanished, with her, the sense of safety in Silver Creek.

Would the night that began with promise and excitement end in a void of unanswered questions and a haunting silence that would forever alter Silver Creek? Clara's disappearance became a mystery cast in shadow, leaving me—and the entire town—on a relentless quest for truth.

That night. That night.

The night of the Harvest Festival, when Clara's disappearance became the vanishing point.

Chapter 1

The Warning

Present day,

The town of Silver Creek lies nestled in the foothills of the Appalachian Mountains, its quaint streets and charming houses bathed in the fading light of early autumn. As the sun dips below the horizon, shadows lengthen, casting a somber veil over the old-fashioned storefronts. The once-gentle murmur of the creek now seems to whisper dark secrets.

Ancient trees loom over narrow streets, twisted branches reaching out like skeletal hands. The air is thick with an eerie stillness, broken only by the rustle of leaves or the distant cry of an unseen creature. Silver

THE VANISHING POINT

Creek feels timeless, yet something unsettles it as if the town is trapped in a perpetual twilight, neither fully alive nor entirely at rest.

I've lived in Silver Creek nearly my entire life, and I always feel the weight of its history. Beneath its picturesque surface, something dark seems to fester, waiting to be uncovered.

At thirty-five, I'm the town's librarian—a position I cherish for the sanctuary it provides and the endless opportunity to lose myself in countless stories. The soft rustle of pages and the faint scent of old books offer me the solace I have yet to find elsewhere.

The autumn sun caught my auburn hair, each strand glinting as the wind playfully tugged at my tightly secured ponytail. Unlike my unruly hair, determined to escape its bounds, my sharp mind and unwavering resolve were constants, traits others often remarked upon. On that particular day, as I navigated the bustling streets, my clear blue eyes absorbed every detail, scanning for any sign of the unexpected.

It wasn't just any other day; it was one where every sense was heightened, and every decision felt significant.

I sat in the quiet solitude of the garden, a delicate porcelain cup of tea cradled in my hands. The air was crisp with the scent of blooming roses and freshly cut grass — a stark contrast to the heaviness that weighed on my heart. As I took a sip, the warmth brought fleeting comfort, but my thoughts wandered far beyond the garden's peaceful façade.

My mind drifted to Clara — my sister, my closest companion in childhood — and the inexplicable loss that had defined my life for the past decade. Memories of our shared moments played in my mind like scenes from an old film: her infectious laughter ringing out, our mischievous adventures, and the innocent dreams we once shared.

Clara was always the spirited one, with a radiant smile that could light up the darkest room. Her auburn curls cascaded down her back, framing her face with striking green eyes that sparkled with curiosity and mischief. A sprinkle of freckles across her nose and cheeks added to her youthful charm, and her energy was boundless, like a whirlwind of joy that left everyone around her enchanted. The vision of her, so vivid and full of life, made her absence all the more unbearable.

I vividly remembered the day our mother placed Clara's hand in mine, her voice a mix of affection and worry. "Take care of her," she had said, her eyes full of maternal concern. "She's little, and she's careless." Those words, once a gentle reminder, now echoed with an unbearable weight.

Clara's disappearance shattered my peace, leaving behind a void that time has yet to fill. The ache in my heart was as raw as it had been on that fateful day when she vanished without a trace. Five years had passed since then, but the pain and uncertainty remained as intense as ever. I had searched tirelessly, hoping to find some clue, some sign of her fate, but each lead only brought disappointment and despair. As I sat there, enveloped in memories and the quiet rustling of leaves, I couldn't escape the gnawing uncertainty that plagued me. What had happened to Clara that day? Where had she gone? Was she safe, somewhere beyond my reach, or had something terrible befallen her?

The garden, usually a place of solace, offered no answers—only the gentle sway of branches and the distant chirping of birds. The sun cast dappled shadows across the path before me, a poignant reminder of the shadows that had clouded my life since Clara's disappearance.

Lost in thought, I gripped the teacup tighter, seeking comfort in its warmth. But no matter how hard I tried to push the questions aside, they persisted, taunting me with their unresolved mysteries. Clara's absence had left a void that nothing could fill—a wound that time had failed to heal, leaving me adrift in a sea of unanswered questions and lingering grief.

When I felt overwhelmed, as I often did in these moments of quiet reflection, I sought refuge in the library. Books had been my companions since childhood, their pages offering escape, knowledge, and a sense of order absent in the chaos of life. So, with a heavy heart and a mind full of turmoil, I found myself drawn to that familiar haven once more.

THE VANISHING POINT

I reluctantly set the now-cold teacup down on the garden table; its warmth long faded, unnoticed in my contemplation. It dawned on me that I had been lost in thought longer than I realized, my mind consumed by memories of Clara. With a sigh, I pushed my chair back, its legs scraping softly against the gravel, and rose to my feet.

Leaving the garden behind, I retraced familiar paths toward the library. Each step felt heavy, burdened with the weight of unanswered questions and the ache of unresolved grief. The air around me seemed thickened by the emotions I struggled to contain.

As I approached the library, its imposing oak doors loomed before me. I reached out, fingers brushing the cool metal of the handle, and pulled it open with a soft creak. Stepping inside, I was greeted by the familiar scent of aged paper and polished wood — an aroma that never failed to calm me.

The library was a place frozen in time, a sanctuary where the outside world's chaos could be momentarily left behind. Sunlight filtered through tall windows, casting long shadows across the rows of shelves filled with countless volumes. The silence within was palpable, broken only by the soft shuffle of my footsteps on the worn carpet.

I walked down the aisles, my hand grazing the spines of books I knew well, seeking solace in their silent wisdom. Each book held a story of its own, a narrative waiting to be discovered—a parallel to my own quest for understanding and closure.

Here, in the quiet solitude, I found a semblance of peace. The library offered me not just escape but a chance to confront the turmoil within me.

With each book I touched, I felt connected to a world beyond my own—a world where answers, however elusive, might yet be found. But no matter how deeply I delved into the comfort of my literary refuge, Clara's absence remained an unhealed wound, a mystery lingering like a ghost in the quiet corners of my mind.

As I settled at my desk, the morning light streaming through stained glass windows, a familiar figure appeared at the door. Robert Sullivan—a tall, rugged man with a perpetual five o'clock shadow and eyes that missed nothing—walked in with a purposeful stride. His dark, slightly tousled hair added to his look of casual intensity, while his square jaw and broad shoulders lent him an imposing presence. Dressed in his usual worn leather jacket and jeans, he exuded a no-nonsense demeanor, with a quiet confidence that commanded respect.

I first met Robert the day I went to the police station to report Clara's disappearance. The station buzzed with activity, amplifying my already heightened anxiety. As I explained my sister's situation to the officer on duty, I noticed a man nearby, listening closely.

When I finished, he approached me. "I'm Robert Sullivan," he introduced himself. "I was here visiting a friend on the force and overheard your story. I'm a private detective, and I think I can help you find your sister." His voice was gravelly yet warm, carrying a sense of quiet confidence that immediately put me at ease.

Seeing the desperation in my eyes, Robert stepped outside with me. "I heard you mention your financial issues," he said sincerely. "This case is sensitive—it's about a girl's life. I want to help you. I'll charge a nominal fee because I believe this is important."

In that moment, Robert felt like a godsend. Desperate and clinging to a glimmer of hope, I checked his detective license, verifying his credentials. His offer seemed like a lifeline, and I agreed to let him take on the case.

From that point on, Robert became a crucial part of my life. His relentless pursuit of leads and unwavering determination gave me the strength I needed to keep going. More than just a professional ally, he became a confidant and a source of support during those dark days.

Seeing him now after so long stirred a mix of emotions within me—the past and present colliding in the quiet sanctuary of my library.

I smiled, curiosity sparking in my expression as Robert greeted me with his gravelly yet warm voice.

"Morning, Amanda."

"Morning, Robert. To what do I owe the pleasure?"

My mind raced with possibilities. It was unusual to see him here after so long, and my curiosity grew. My heart skipped a beat, hoping he might bring good news—maybe he had found my lost sister. His unexpected visit made me wonder what could be so important.

Robert returned to his desk after years abroad to find two letters waiting for him—silent witnesses to his unfinished business with Clara's case. We had worked together for three years searching for Clara until his mother fell severely ill and had to be admitted to a hospital overseas. I urged him to prioritize her care; her life was just as important. He left, and once his mother recovered, he returned. Now, these letters posed more questions than answers.

Why now? Why had they surfaced after years of silence? And who had sent them, ensuring they would land directly in his hands upon his return?

The letters hinted at secrets buried deep, with

references to places and names long forgotten. Robert studied them meticulously, searching for clues that might lead him closer to the truth behind Clara's disappearance. The urgency to solve the case gnawed at him, driven not only by professional duty but by the personal connection forged through years of relentless pursuit.

Our meeting was pivotal. As we spoke, memories of Clara painted vivid scenes in both our minds—fragments of a life interrupted, a family shattered by loss. He sensed my guarded hope, tempered by years of disappointment and uncertainty.

In my hesitant words and haunted eyes, Robert saw reflections of his own determination. As we delved deeper, he couldn't shake the feeling that someone else knew more than they were letting on. Shadows of suspicion fell on old acquaintances and forgotten leads. The journey to uncovering the truth was fraught with twists and turns, testing both Robert's resolve and his courage.

Yet, amidst the uncertainty, Robert found his purpose renewed—a commitment to justice that transcended time and distance. With me by his side, he embarked on a quest for answers, determined not only to bring closure to Clara's case but also to heal the wounds that had scarred our lives for far too long.

Robert hesitated momentarily before reaching into his coat pocket. "I received these letters and thought you should see them." He handed me a plain white envelope, my name scrawled on it in an unfamiliar hand.

My heart skipped a beat as I took the envelope, a sense of foreboding settling over me. Carefully, I opened it, unfolding a single sheet of paper. The message was brief yet chilling:

"She's still alive. Find her before it's too late.

The words seemed to pulsate on the page, each one hammering against my heart. I looked up at Robert, my eyes wide with shock. "Is this some kind of sick joke?"

Robert shook his head. "I don't think so. I received a similar note. No postmark, no return address. Just this." He showed me his note, which read:

"You failed once. Don't fail again."

My mind raced. Could Clara really be alive after all these years? It seemed impossible, yet the note's urgency was undeniable. Barely above a whisper, I asked him, "What do we do?"

"We start by figuring out who sent these and why," Robert replied, his jaw set in determination. "I'll look into any recent cases or reports that might be related. You should check the library archives for anything that stands out. Maybe we missed something."

I nodded, already considering where to begin. The library held decades of town records, newspapers, and documents that might offer a clue. As Robert left, I turned toward the archive room, my heart pounding with a mix of fear and hope.

Hours passed as I sifted through old newspapers and files, my eyes scanning for anything that might connect to Clara's disappearance. The silence of the library, usually comforting, now felt oppressive, with the ticking clock on the wall a constant reminder of time slipping away.

Just as I began to feel overwhelmed, a headline from an old issue of the Silver Creek Gazette caught my eye: "Local Girl Disappears without a Trace." It was dated five years ago, the day after Clara vanished. I read through the article, lingering over details I knew by heart—the description of Clara, the timeline of her last known movements, the futile search efforts.

Then, something new: a mention of a witness who had come forward a week after Clara's disappearance. A man named Henry Lawson claimed to have seen a suspicious figure near the creek the night Clara went missing. The article noted that Lawson's statement had been dismissed due to a lack of evidence and his reputation as the town drunk.

My pulse quickened. I had never heard of Henry Lawson before. Could he hold the key to finding Clara? I jotted down his name and address from the article, deciding to pay him a visit.

As I gathered my belongings to leave the library, a thought struck me: what if someone didn't want Clara to be found? The notes hinted at urgency—and danger. I glanced around the library, a sudden sense of vulnerability creeping over me. Taking a deep breath, I reminded myself that I was doing this for Clara and wouldn't be deterred.

The sun was beginning to set as I drove toward the outskirts of town where Henry Lawson lived. The road wound through dense woods, shadows stretching long and menacing. At last, I arrived at a small, rundown cabin, its windows dark and uninviting.

Steeling myself, I knocked on the door. After a long moment, it creaked open, revealing a gaunt, elderly man with piercing eyes. In a raspy voice, he asked, "What do you want?"

"Mr. Lawson? My name is Amanda Crater. I'm looking for information about my sister, Clara. She disappeared five years ago, and I read that you might have seen something."

Henry Lawson, a wiry man in his late sixties, peered at me through thick, round glasses. His thinning gray hair was neatly combed, and deep lines etched across his forehead and around his mouth hinted at a life filled with hardships. His eyes, a faded blue, held a glimmer of sharpness alongside a hint of wary curiosity. Dressed in a threadbare cardigan and faded slacks, he looked like someone who had seen too much and trusted too little. As he shifted, I noticed his calloused, weathered hands clasped tightly together, concealing the tension he felt.

Lawson's eyes narrowed. "Why now? Why after all these years?"

"Because I believe she's still alive," I replied, my voice trembling with a mix of hope and desperation. "Please, if you know anything, tell me."

Lawson stared at me for what felt like an eternity before nodding slowly. "Come in," he said, stepping aside. "There's something you need to know."

As I stepped into the dimly lit cabin, a wave of foreboding mingled with determination. I was on the brink of uncovering a truth that had eluded me for years, and I wouldn't stop until I found my sister.

The warning had been given, and the hunt was on.

Chapter 2

Silent Unseen Connections

Henry Lawson's cabin was musty and dim, a place that seemed to hold secrets in every shadow. The air was thick with the scent of damp wood and old memories, making me feel as if I'd stepped back in time.

I followed him into the small living room, where he motioned for me to sit on a threadbare couch that looked like it had seen better days decades ago. As I settled onto the sagging cushions, a faint cloud of dust rose around me. Henry took his seat in an old armchair across from me, its fabric worn thin and patched in places. His gaze remained fixed on my face, intense and searching, as if he were trying to gauge my intentions.

I asked Henry, "What do you remember from

that night?" I struggled to keep my voice steady despite the anxiety gnawing at me. My palms were sweaty, and I discreetly wiped them on my jeans.

Henry took a deep breath, his eyes growing distant as he recalled the events. "I was by the creek late at night. It was too late for anyone to be out, really, but I couldn't sleep, and the creek has always been my place to think. The moon was just a sliver in the sky, casting long shadows that danced on the water's surface. I saw someone—I couldn't make out who—dragging something heavy toward the water. It was dark, and I was too far away to see clearly. When I got closer, they were gone, and so was whatever they had been carrying. The whole scene felt like something out of a nightmare—hazy and unreal."

My heart pounded in my chest. "Why didn't you come forward sooner? Why wasn't this investigated properly?" My voice betrayed my frustration, even as I tried to keep it in check. The mystery had gnawed at the edges of my thoughts for so long, and now, hearing Henry's account, I felt a mix of anger and desperation.

Henry's eyes flickered with a mix of shame and defensiveness. He spoke quietly, "I tried to tell someone, but no one believed me. They thought I was just a crazy old man, imagining things. The sheriff barely listened, and after a while, I just gave up. What was the point in pushing if no one would take me seriously?"

I could see the pain in his eyes, the weight of unspoken truths and ignored warnings. The small room seemed to close in around us, the walls bearing silent witness to Henry's isolation and despair. This was more than just a simple account of events; it was a cry for validation, a desperate need to be heard and believed. I knew I had to handle this carefully — not just for the investigation, but for Henry's fragile sense of self-worth.

Henry sighed deeply, the sound heavy with decades of unspoken truths. "This town has its secrets, Miss Amanda. There have always been rumors and whispers of things that happen in the shadows. I've kept my distance, but I've heard enough to know that not everything is as it seems. You need to be careful."

His words sent a chill down my spine — a cold shiver that began at the nape of my neck and worked its way down. But they also ignited a fierce determination within me. "Thank you, Mr. Lawson. I'll be careful, but I have to find out what happened to my sister Clara." The name hung in the air between us, heavy with loss and unanswered questions.

As I left the cabin, the sun had fully set, and the woods around me felt oppressive in their darkness. The trees seemed to close in, their branches reaching out like skeletal fingers. The only sounds were the crunch of leaves underfoot and the distant hoot of an owl. I drove back to Silver Creek, my mind racing with possibilities. Henry's account was the first new lead in years, giving me a direction, however vague.

The road back was winding and narrow, flanked by dense forest that pressed in on all sides. The headlights of my car sliced through the darkness, revealing glimpses of nocturnal creatures that scurried away from the sudden intrusion of light.

My thoughts were a jumble of fear and hope, the weight of the past pressing heavily on my shoulders.

The next morning, I met Robert at the diner, the only place in town that opened early enough for our impromptu meetings. The diner was a relic from a bygone era, featuring red vinyl booths and a jukebox that hadn't worked in years. The smell of bacon and freshly brewed coffee filled the air, providing a comforting contrast to the tension gnawing at my insides. He was already seated at our usual booth, a steaming cup of coffee in front of him.

Robert looked up as I approached, his eyes tired but alert. He was one of the few people I could trust in this town. "Morning, Amanda," he greeted, sliding a menu across the table, though we both knew I'd order the usual. "You look like you've seen a ghost."

I slid into the booth opposite him, trying to muster a smile. "I might have, in a way. I talked to Henry Lawson last night."

Robert raised an eyebrow, his interest piqued. "And?"

"He saw something the night Clara disappeared—something that might finally give us a clue." I recounted Henry's story, watching Robert's expression shift from skepticism to cautious interest.

When I finished, he leaned back in his seat, rubbing his chin thoughtfully. "If Henry's telling the truth—and there's no reason to think he isn't—we might be onto something. But we have to be careful. There are people in this town who don't want the past dredged up."

His warning echoed Henry's, and I nodded, feeling the weight of their words. "I know. But I can't let it go, Robert. I need to know what happened to Clara. For her sake and for mine."

He sighed, a resigned smile touching his lips. "Alright, Amanda. Let's see where this leads. But remember, some secrets are buried for a reason. Digging them up can be dangerous. We need to be careful; your safety and Clara's is my priority."

As we made plans to investigate further, I couldn't shake the feeling that we were on the brink of something significant—something that could change everything. The diner's warm, familiar surroundings suddenly felt like a fragile bubble, protecting us from the dark truths lurking just beyond its doors.

I recounted my conversation with Henry. Robert listened intently, his expression growing more serious with every word. The clinking of utensils and the murmur of conversations around us faded into the background as we delved deeper into the mystery.

"We need to talk to the sheriff," he said once I finished, his voice resolute. "We should see if there's any record of Henry's statement, and if not, find out why."

We walked over to the sheriff's office, a small, unassuming building on Main Street. It was one of those places you could pass a hundred times without really noticing, yet it held the authority of the law in our town. Sheriff Bennett, a grizzled man with a no-nonsense demeanor, greeted us with a raised eyebrow.

His salt-and-pepper hair was cut short, and his weathered face bore the marks of countless long days and even longer nights. His piercing gray eyes held a steely resolve, tempered by a hint of tiredness that spoke of years spent dealing with the town's troubles. Clad in a neatly pressed uniform, complete with a sheriff's badge gleaming on his chest, he radiated stern authority. Despite his rough exterior, there was an underlying sense of duty and commitment to his community that was impossible to ignore.

"Well, what brings you two here?" he asked, leaning back in his chair, his voice a mix of curiosity and weariness.

Robert spoke first. "Sheriff, we need to revisit the case of Clara Crater. Specifically, a statement given by Henry Lawson shortly after her disappearance."

The sheriff's expression hardened, and the lines on his face deepened. "That case was closed a long time ago. Lawson's a known drunk. His statement was unreliable." His tone was dismissive, as if the matter were not worth revisiting.

I stepped forward, my voice firm and steady. "With all due respect, Sheriff, my sister's case was never truly closed. We've received new information suggesting she might still be alive. We need to re-examine everything, starting with Lawson's statement." The words felt heavy, laden with years of unanswered questions and unresolved grief.

Sheriff Bennett sighed, rubbing his temples as if

warding off a headache. "Fine. I'll pull the files. But don't get your hopes up. This town has been through enough." His reluctance was palpable, but he rose and walked to the back office.

As we waited for the sheriff to retrieve the documents, I couldn't help but feel a mix of hope and frustration. This was a small step, but it was a step nonetheless. The sterile smell of the office, the humming of the fluorescent lights, and the quiet ticking of the clock on the wall only heightened my anxiety.

When he returned, Sheriff Bennett handed us a thin folder. "This is all we have: Lawson's statement, some notes from the investigation—nothing much." His tone was almost apologetic, as if he understood how little this might mean in the grand scheme of things.

I opened the folder, my heart sinking as I scanned the sparse contents. Henry's statement was there, but it was brief and dismissive, clearly not taken seriously. There were a few notes about the search efforts, but nothing pointed to any new leads. The paper felt flimsy in my hands, and the ink had faded with time, but the significance of these documents was immense.

Robert looked at me with determination in his eyes. "We'll find her, Amanda. We're just getting started." His confidence was reassuring, a beacon in the fog of uncertainty.

The sheriff's stern voice sliced through the stale air of the small, dimly lit office. "It's time to close up now. You need to leave." His tone was final, leaving no room for argument. He sighed, pulling a stack of yellowed papers from a drawer and handing us the copied documents.

"If you need more information, take this file," he muttered, his eyes not quite meeting ours. As we accepted the papers, he leaned in slightly, his voice dropping to a conspiratorial murmur. "It's just a waste of time to explore the case after so long."

His words hung heavy in the air, laden with an unspoken warning. The case had been cold for years, and the trail had long since gone cold, but there was something in his tone — a mixture of resignation and frustration—that made me wonder what he wasn't saying.

We stepped out into the night, the chill seeping into our bones. The file felt like a lead weight in my hands; its significance was not lost on me. Every page, every faded photograph, and every cryptic note was a fragment of a forgotten puzzle—pieces of a mystery that had never been solved.

I glanced back at the sheriff's office, now cloaked in darkness, unable to shake the feeling that we were on the verge of something big—something that someone didn't want us to uncover. The sheriff's words echoed in my mind: a waste of time.

But the truth had a way of clawing its way to the surface, no matter how deeply it was buried. As I flipped through the brittle pages under the dim streetlights, I knew we were about to unearth secrets that some wished had stayed hidden.

Leaving the sheriff's office, the streets of Silver Creek seemed unchanged, but to me, everything looked different. Each face in the crowd, every passerby, seemed like they might hold a piece of the puzzle.

"Where to next?" Robert asked, falling into step beside me.

I thought of Henry's account. "If someone was there that night, they might have left something behind. We need to talk to a few more people who were around back then."

Robert nodded. "I'll gather any supplies we need that might help us find clues."

As we parted ways, I felt a renewed sense of purpose. The road ahead was long and fraught with challenges, but I knew we were on the right track. The answers were out there, waiting to be uncovered, and I was more determined than ever to find them.

I closed the folder, feeling it was a key — one that might finally unlock the secrets that had haunted me for so long. A childhood memory with my sister Clara came flooding back. We often played hide and seek, and one day she hid so cleverly that I couldn't find her. I searched everywhere, from our cluttered attic to the shadowy corners of our basement, but Clara was nowhere to be seen. Time seemed to stretch endlessly as I hunted for her, my frustration growing with each passing minute.

Finally, Clara emerged from a place I could never have imagined—the dark, ghostly backyard of our home. It was a place I dreaded, with its gnarled trees and creeping vines casting eerie shadows, even in daylight. But Clara stepped out of the darkness without a hint of fear, her face calm and serene.

"Clara, why did you go there?" My voice trembled with a mix of relief and lingering fear. "Aren't you scared of the ghosts?"

She looked at me with a mixture of amusement and pity. "Come on, there's nothing like that." A small, knowing smile graced her face. "That place is dark and calm, not scary at all."

Her words were strange and unsettling, as if she saw the world through a different lens—one that stripped away fear and replaced it with tranquility. I couldn't understand how she could be so at ease in a place that made my skin crawl.

As we stood there, Clara's demeanor shifted. She grew serious, her eyes boring into mine with an intensity that took me aback. "Amanda, if I ever got lost one day and you couldn't find me, like today, would you forget about me? Would you stop looking for me?"

Her question hit me like a punch to the gut. I saw a flicker of vulnerability in her eyes, a rare glimpse into emotions she usually kept hidden. The thought of losing her, even in a game, was unbearable. My throat tightened as I felt a surge of emotion mirroring her own.

"Never," I replied, my voice thick with conviction. "I would never stop looking for you, Clara. I'd find you, no matter what."

Clara's eyes softened, and she gave me a small, sad smile. "Promise?"

I wrapped her in my arms and said, "Promise." In that moment, I felt a deep, unspoken bond between us — a promise that went beyond words.

Years later, whenever I found myself standing alone in that same ghostly backyard, the memory of that day haunted me. Clara had disappeared, not in a game of hide and seek but in the cruel, unforgiving reality of life. I had searched for her tirelessly, holding onto the promise I made, but she remained lost — a shadow in the dark corners of my mind.

I was lost in the depths of my memories when Robert's voice jolted me back to reality. "What are you thinking so deeply? Are you okay?"

I blinked, shaking off the lingering ghosts of the past as I sat up in the car. My reply was barely above a whisper: "No, Robert. I just drifted back to a time with my sister. I made her a promise — to always find her and keep her safe, no matter what. But I failed her. I didn't keep that promise. I feel like a terrible sister."

Tears welled up in my eyes, threatening to spill over. I clenched my fists, fighting to keep my emotions in check. Robert reached over, his hand warm and reassuring on my shoulder.

"Amanda," he said gently, meeting my gaze with unwavering support. "You're not a terrible sister. You've done everything in your power, and you're still fighting for her. We will find her. I promise you that. I'll be with you every step of the way."

His words were a lifeline, pulling me out of the

despair that threatened to consume me. In his eyes, I saw the strength and determination I needed to keep going. For Clara and the promise that still bound us, I would never stop searching. With Robert by my side, I knew I wouldn't have to face the darkness alone.

A sense of purpose filled me. Clara's trail had gone cold, but it wasn't impossible to follow. I'd spent five years waiting for answers; now it was time to find them. Each step away from the sheriff's office felt like a step closer to the truth.

Robert dropped me off at the library, the weight of our conversation still heavy on my mind. As I stepped out of the car, I turned to him, my voice steady but urgent. "Robert, take some rest and then get back to me with the details. We need to keep moving forward."

He nodded, his expression serious yet supportive. "I will, Amanda. I'll gather everything we need and be in touch soon." With a final, reassuring squeeze of my hand, he watched me walk into the library.

After I went inside the library, I began my

search through the archives, looking for any mention of suspicious activity around the time Clara disappeared. Despite my exhaustion, I continued to explore the library. The familiar scent of old books and polished wood had always been a source of comfort, but now it felt like a battleground for uncovering hidden truths.

Sifting through yellowed pages and faded ink was painstaking work, yet I was driven by a relentless need to find the truth. Each article and report felt like a piece of a vast puzzle I was determined to solve.

Then, another clue emerged. An old newspaper clipping about a series of break-ins that occurred in the months leading up to Clara's disappearance caught my eye. The headline, though faded, was clear enough: "Series of Unsolved Break-Ins Baffles Town." One of the houses broken into belonged to the mayor at the time, a man named Richard Hargrove.

According to the article, nothing of value was taken, but a sense of unease lingered in the community. Residents had become wary, locking their doors earlier and casting suspicious glances at strangers.

I jotted down the details, my mind racing with questions. Could there be a connection between the break-ins and Clara's disappearance? The timing seemed too coincidental to ignore. I needed to learn more about Richard Hargrove and his possible ties to the case. The mayor's name had come up before, but this new context sharpened my focus.

Unable to concentrate, I decided to call Robert again. "Robert, we need to meet Richard Hargrove," I said, urgency clear in my voice.

There was a pause before he responded, "You're right. Let's meet him first thing tomorrow. But Amanda, you need to rest. Tomorrow morning at exactly 8 a.m., I'll be with you, and we'll go see Richard Hargrove together."

I sighed, feeling exhaustion seep into my bones. "Okay, Robert. I'll try to get some rest."

"Good," he replied, his voice reassuring. "We'll get through this, Amanda. Together."

I hung up, feeling a glimmer of hope amidst the fatigue. As the night turned into morning, I met Robert again to share my findings. He listened carefully, nodding as I spoke. "Hargrove's still around. He's retired but remains a prominent figure in town. We should talk to him," Robert suggested, his eyes reflecting the same determination that fueled my own resolve.

We made our way to Hargrove's house, a stately old home on the outskirts of town. The house stood out among the more modest dwellings, its grandeur a testament to Hargrove's long-standing influence. The former mayor greeted us with a mixture of curiosity and apprehension. His hair, now silver, added an air of wisdom, but his eyes held a flicker of guardedness.

Robert began explaining our purpose. His voice was calm yet firm, conveying both respect and urgency. "Mr. Hargrove, we're looking into some old cases."

Hargrove's expression darkened, and the lines on his face deepened. "Clara Crater's disappearance? That was a tragedy. But why bring it up now?" His voice was thick with memories, some perhaps better left untouched. Though tall and slender, he retained an imposing presence, carrying himself with a dignity that hinted at his years in public service. Dressed in a well-tailored suit, he exuded an air of sophistication, yet tension radiated from him, as if the weight of past secrets bore heavily upon his shoulders.

After observing his reaction closely, I said, "We've received new information suggesting she might still be alive." His eyes widened slightly, and his posture stiffened. "We also read about the break-ins around the same time. Do you think there could be a connection?"

Hargrove hesitated, his gaze shifting away. It was a fleeting moment, but one that spoke volumes. "I don't know. Those were strange times. But if it helps find Clara, I'll do whatever I can." His voice was earnest, yet an undercurrent of something unspoken lingered in the air.

We questioned him about the break-ins, but his answers were vague, shrouded in the fog of years past. He recounted the events with a detached air, as if telling an old, half-forgotten story. Still, a sense of something unspoken lingered, a hint that he might know more than he was willing to share. His eyes flickered with brief moments of hesitation, as if weighing how much to reveal.

As we left Hargrove's house, Robert turned to me, his brow furrowed in thought. "There's more to this, Amanda. We just need to keep digging." His words were both a challenge and a promise, a vow to uncover the truth, no matter how deeply it was buried.

I nodded, feeling the weight of the mystery pressing down on me. The pieces were starting to come together, but the picture they formed remained unclear. Each new discovery brought more questions, yet also the hope of answers just within reach. I wouldn't stop—not until I found Clara.

As I drove home that night, the streets of Silver Creek bathed in the pale glow of the moon, I knew the search had only just begun. The town, with its quiet facade, held more secrets than I had ever imagined. I was ready for whatever lay ahead. The road was long, and the night was dark, but my resolve was unwavering. Clara's story was far from over, and so

THE VANISHING POINT

was my quest to find her.

Chapter 3

A Promise and a Proposal

We had to pause our search. The town announced a festival—a day when everyone set aside their worries to celebrate. It felt like a cruel twist of fate, halting our momentum just as we were gaining traction in our relentless pursuit of answers. For me, it was disheartening; the weight of Clara's disappearance pressed heavily on my shoulders. Each passing day without answers felt like another knot tightening in my chest, suffocating hope with every breath.

Robert noticed my despair, his concern palpable in the gentle touch of his hand on mine. His voice, usually steady and reassuring, now carried a hint of uncertainty as he tried to lift my spirits. "Amanda, perhaps this could be a blessing in disguise. A chance for us to clear our minds and gather our thoughts before diving back into the shadows."

His words echoed with bitter irony, yet there was wisdom in them. Despite my reluctance to join in the festivities, I couldn't ignore the solace found in Robert's presence. Amidst the vibrant colors and cheerful laughter of the festival, our worries momentarily faded into the background. Still, the unresolved mystery of Clara's whereabouts gnawed at our resolve, reminding us that our respite was temporary.

"Come on, Amanda," he urged, his voice now a soothing balm to my troubled thoughts. "Let's go to the festival. It might do us good to take a break, even if it's just for a few hours."

Reluctantly, I agreed. With a heavy heart and weary steps, I followed Robert into the heart of the festivities. The town square was alive with color and sound, a kaleidoscope of laughter and music that felt so distant from the darkness we were entrenched in.

Stalls lined the streets, offering everything from handmade crafts to savory treats that filled the air with tantalizing aromas. Children ran around with sticky fingers and wide smiles, their innocence a stark contrast to the shadows lurking in my mind.

Robert guided me through the crowd, his presence a steady anchor in the sea of faces. Unlike the festival's cheer, he seemed unaffected, his focus unwavering as if he had a purpose beyond mere distraction.

As we strolled past a row of booths, Robert suddenly stopped in front of a fortune teller's tent. A sign proclaimed, "See Your Future Unveiled." I hesitated, skeptical of such things, but Robert's eyes twinkled with mischief. He leaned closer and teased softly, "Come on, Amanda. Let's see what the future holds for us."

With a sigh, I relented, allowing him to lead me inside. The fortune teller, a woman with wise eyes and a knowing smile, beckoned us to sit. Her gaze lingered on us, as if she could sense the weight of our burdens.

She took my hand first, tracing the lines with delicate fingers. Her voice was low and melodious as she spoke. "You are searching for someone, lost in the shadows. But your journey is not just about finding her; it is also about finding yourself in the process."

Her words struck a chord within me, resonating with the doubts and fears I had buried deep. Robert's hand tightened around mine, offering silent reassurance

Then it was Robert's turn. The fortune teller studied his palm with intense concentration before meeting his gaze. "You carry a heavy burden, Robert," she murmured, her voice grave. "But love will be your guiding light. It will lead you through the darkest nights and into the dawn of a new day."

Robert glanced at me, a smile tugging at the corners of his lips. "Thank you," he said softly to the fortune teller, his tone sincere. As we left the tent, the evening sun cast a golden hue over the festival, painting everything with a warm glow. Music drifted through the air, mingling with the laughter of children and the chatter of townsfolk.

Robert led me away from the fortune teller's tent, and I couldn't help but feel a mix of curiosity and excitement. The bustling crowd engulfed us, their laughter and chatter blending into a vibrant symphony of voices. I glanced around, trying to decipher where Robert was taking me amidst the sea of people.

We maneuvered through the lively throng until we suddenly emerged into a clearing at the center of the festival grounds. My breath caught as I beheld a stunning sight: a large heart outlined on the ground with delicate rose petals, its vibrant red hue contrasting beautifully with the green grass beneath our feet. In the center of the heart was a small table adorned with a cake decorated with intricate frosting hearts and candles flickering gently in the afternoon breeze.

I whispered to Robert, glancing around at the bustling crowd, "What is all this? It feels like we've stumbled upon someone's private, beautifully decorated proposal setup. Why did you bring me here?" My voice was barely audible over the festive atmosphere, filled with a mix of curiosity and wonder.

Robert smiled, his eyes sparkling with a blend of tenderness and nervous anticipation. "Amanda," he began, gently touching my hand, "I wanted this moment to be special. To show you how much you mean to me."

I gazed at him, my heart suddenly pounding with a whirlwind of emotions. This unexpected gesture amidst the chaos of the festival touched me deeply, a poignant reminder of how much Robert understood and cared for me.

I caught sight of a table where a large cake sat, adorned with elegant frosting that spelled out "Amanda, I love you." Beside it was a beautifully inscribed card with my name delicately written, surrounded by even more rose petals. "It's not just any festival, Amanda. It's a day to celebrate us."

Tears welled in my eyes as I absorbed the thoughtful details Robert had orchestrated. The warmth of his love enveloped me like a comforting embrace, soothing the ache that had lingered since Clara's disappearance.

"You've done all this for me?" I murmured, overwhelmed by the depth of his affection.

Robert nodded, his expression earnest. "I wanted to create a moment of joy for us amidst everything else. To remind you that even in uncertainty, there's beauty and love."

I stepped closer, feeling the gentle tug of his presence drawing me in. The noise of the festival faded into the background, leaving only the two of us in our own world within the heart of roses

"And now," Robert said, his voice tinged with a hint of nervousness, "there's one more thing."

Before I could comprehend his words, he knelt beside the table, his eyes never leaving mine. My heart skipped a beat as he reached into his pocket and produced a small velvet box. Gasps and whispers rippled through the crowd as they realized what was unfolding before them.

With trembling hands, Robert opened the box to reveal a shimmering ring nestled within. "Amanda," he said, his voice steady despite the emotions shimmering in his eyes, "will you marry me?"

Time seemed to stand still as I gazed at the man before me — the one who had stood by my side through uncertainty and fear — now laying bare his heart in the most vulnerable of gestures. The world around us faded away, leaving only the echo of his question hanging between us, heavy with hope and possibility.

"Yes," I finally whispered, my voice thick with emotion. "Yes, Robert, a thousand times yes."

Cheers erupted from the crowd, mingling with the pounding of my heart as Robert slipped the ring onto my finger. In that moment, amidst the festival's exuberance and the beauty of his proposal, I knew that no matter what challenges lay ahead, we would face them together, bound by a love that had weathered storms and now shone brighter than ever in the heart of a rose petal-strewn celebration.

He stepped closer, reaching for my hand. "I love you, Amanda," he confessed, his voice thick with emotion. "And I promise you, no matter what happens, I'll be by your side. We'll find Clara together, and when we do, it'll be a gift from me to you… for our future."

Tears welled in my eyes, a mix of gratitude and love swelling in my chest. Surrounded by the bustle of the festival and the promise of tomorrow, I realized our bond had deepened in ways words could never fully capture.

"I love you too, Robert," I whispered, my voice trembling with emotion. "Thank you... for everything."

We stood there, enveloped in each other's embrace, amid the swirl of music and laughter. The weight of our shared purpose felt lighter, buoyed by the strength of our love and determination.

As the festival continued around us, I felt a renewed sense of hope. The journey ahead was uncertain, but with Robert beside me, I knew we could face whatever darkness awaited. Our love had become a beacon, guiding us through the shadows toward a future where Clara's light would shine once more.

And so, hand in hand, we walked into the night, ready to resume our search with renewed vigor and a deeper understanding of what truly mattered. This moment, amidst the festivities and declarations of love, marked the beginning of a new chapter — not just in our quest for Clara, but in our journey together — a journey fueled by love, hope, and the unwavering promise of tomorrow.

Chapter 4

Clues in the Dark

That night, sleep eluded me. Despite the warmth of Robert's proposal and the hope it instilled, the unresolved mystery of Clara's disappearance gnawed at my mind. As I lay in bed, I replayed every detail Henry Lawson had shared, every word from Sheriff Bennett and Richard Hargrove. Clara's absence felt closer yet frustratingly out of reach. What had I missed? What connections had I yet to uncover? The questions swirled in my mind, refusing to let me rest.

I turned onto my side, the engagement ring Robert had given me catching the moonlight. It sparkled—a beacon of love and commitment, a reminder that amidst the darkness, I wasn't alone. I clutched the ring, finding solace in its presence. "I am not alone in this journey," I consoled myself. "Now, I have found the best person I trust. If God has sent Robert to me, He will also lead me to my sister. I trust in God's blessings. It may be late, but we will surely get there."

The next morning, I woke up groggy but determined. Robert's love had given me new strength and a renewed sense of purpose. I needed to dive back into the archives and find the missing pieces of this puzzle. As I arrived at the library early, a sense of urgency coursed through me. I needed to get ahead and uncover something—anything—that could lead me to Clara. The memory of Robert's proposal the previous night bolstered my resolve. His love and support were unwavering, and now more than ever, I felt determined to uncover the truth.

Unlocking the door to the library, I was greeted by an unexpected sight. There, wedged in the frame, was a folded piece of paper. My heart pounded as I reached for it, a mix of fear and anticipation coursing through me. Who left this? And why? With trembling hands, I unfolded the note. The message was short but chilling: "Time is running out. Don't trust everyone." I stared at the words, my mind racing. "Who could have written this?" I whispered to myself, the weight of the warning settling over me.

Determined to get to the bottom of this, I slipped the note into my pocket and headed straight for the archives. There was no time to waste. Clara's fate hung in the balance, and now, more than ever, I needed to uncover the truth.

As I delved into the dusty records, I felt a chill run down my spine. The clock was ticking, and every second brought me closer to—or further from—finding Clara. I had to stay focused, trust my instincts, and hope that, somehow, I would find the answers I desperately needed.

I sat down heavily at my desk, staring at the note. The words seemed to dance on the paper, taunting me with their ambiguity. "Who could have left it?" I wondered aloud, my voice barely more than a whisper in the empty library. "And why? Are they trying to help, or is this a warning to back off?" My mind raced with possibilities, each more unsettling than the last.

I took a deep breath, trying to steady my nerves. The mystery was becoming more complex by the minute, but one thing was clear: I couldn't let fear control me. If anything, this note only strengthened my resolve. "I won't be scared off," I muttered, more to myself than anyone else. "I need to find Clara."

As the morning wore on, Robert joined me, walking in with two steaming cups of coffee. A tender light sparkled in his eyes. "Morning, my love," he said, handing me a cup. "I thought you could use this."

"Thanks, Robert," I replied, feeling a flutter in my chest. Last night, he had proposed, and our relationship had taken a beautiful turn. His presence was more than just comforting; it was a reminder of the love and support we shared. I slid the note across the desk to him and spoke quietly, "We've got a new development."

Robert's eyes scanned the message, and I noticed his jaw tighten. He looked up at me, concern etched on his face. "Someone's trying to mess with us," he said, his voice low and serious. "Or maybe warn us.

THE VANISHING POINT

Either way, we need to be careful."

I nodded, a mix of fear and determination swirling inside me. "We're getting close, Robert. I can feel it. But we can't trust anyone. We need to watch our backs."

Robert took a deep sip of his coffee, then set the cup down with a decisive thud. "Agreed. Let's be smart about this. We'll keep digging, but we won't take any unnecessary risks."

His support bolstered my resolve. "Thanks, Robert. I don't know what I'd do without you."

He reached out, taking my hand and giving it a reassuring squeeze. "We're in this together, Amanda. We'll find Clara. No matter what it takes."

The day ahead would be long and arduous, but I knew we were on the right path. Clara was out there somewhere, and with Robert by my side, I felt a glimmer of hope that we would uncover the truth.

Taking a sip of the coffee, I continued, "I found something about a series of break-ins around the time Clara disappeared. One of the houses was the mayor's. I think there's a connection, but I can't figure out what it is."

Robert nodded thoughtfully. "Let's dig into those break-ins. Maybe there's a pattern we haven't seen."

We spent hours poring over old police reports and newspaper articles, searching for anything that might link the break-ins to Clara's disappearance. It was slow, painstaking work — the kind that tested our patience and resolve. Every piece of paper and every faded headline felt like a potential clue, and we couldn't afford to overlook anything.

As the day dragged on, Robert and I worked in silence, the only sounds being the rustling of papers and the occasional murmur of frustration or discovery. I could feel my eyes straining and my mind growing weary, but I refused to give up. "We're getting closer," I kept telling myself. "Just keep going."

Gradually, a pattern began to emerge. The break-ins had all occurred within a few blocks of each other, clustered around a specific area in town. I traced the locations on an old map, my finger moving from one spot to another. "Robert, look at this," I said, beckoning him over.

He leaned in, studying the map with me. "You're right," his voice tinged with excitement. "They're all so close together. It can't be a coincidence."

Feeling a spark of hope, I added, "Exactly. Each time, nothing of significant value was taken. It's as if the intruder was searching for something specific."

Robert frowned, deep in thought. "But what could they be looking for? And how does it connect to Clara?"

I shook my head, frustration creeping in. "I don't know yet. But there has to be a reason. Maybe Clara had something they wanted, or perhaps she knew something."

We sat back down, poring over the reports with renewed determination. Every detail mattered, no matter how small. I felt like we were on the brink of a breakthrough, but the final piece of the puzzle was still missing.

Looking up at Robert, I suddenly recalled the note. "Remember the note? 'Time is running out. Don't trust everyone.' Maybe it's connected to these break-ins. Someone might be trying to warn us about the same thing."

Robert nodded slowly. "It's possible. We need to dig deeper into the people involved in these reports. There may be a common thread we're not seeing yet."

As we continued our search, Robert found a report that mentioned a name we hadn't seen before: Marcus Hill. He had been a suspect in the break-ins but was never charged due to a lack of evidence. Hill had left town shortly after Clara's disappearance and hadn't been heard from since.

Tapping the report, Robert said, "This is our guy. We need to find Marcus Hill."

We tracked down an address for Hill's last known residence and headed there immediately. The house was a run-down, dilapidated structure on the outskirts of Silver Creek, almost hidden by overgrown weeds and trees. It looked abandoned.

We knocked on the door, but there was no answer. Robert tried the handle, and it swung open with a creak. Inside, the house was a mess—dust and

THE VANISHING POINT

cobwebs everywhere, broken furniture, and scattered papers. It was clear no one had lived here for a long time.

We split up to search the house. As I moved through the dimly lit rooms, a growing sense of unease settled in. In the back, I discovered a small office, its desk cluttered with papers and notebooks. I began sifting through the disarray, hoping to uncover something — anything — that might lead us to Hill.

One of the notebooks caught my eye, its pages filled with cryptic entries referencing "the girl" and "the creek." My heart raced as I realized these entries were about Clara.

"Robert, you need to see this!" I called out.

He joined me in the office, and we pored over the notebook together. The entries were fragmented and disjointed but revealed the unsettling obsession of someone who had been watching Clara. The last entry was dated the very day she disappeared.

"This is it," Robert said, his voice steady but urgent. "We need to find out where Hill went. If he's still alive, he might know where Clara is."

With the notebook tucked safely away, we left the house, our minds racing with new questions. Who was Marcus Hill, really? And what had he done with Clara?

As we drove back to town, we decided to visit the Silver Creek Gazette for any additional information. The newspaper office was a small, cluttered space run by an elderly man named Harold Whitaker, the town's editor for as long as anyone could remember.

Harold was a spry old man with a shock of white hair that seemed perpetually tousled. His round glasses perched precariously on the bridge of his nose, magnifying eyes that remained sharp and inquisitive despite his age. Clad in a well-worn tweed jacket over a sweater vest, he exuded the air of an old-school journalist dedicated to his craft. His fingers were ink-stained from years of handling newspapers, and he moved with deliberate energy—a testament to his unwavering passion for uncovering the truth.

As he welcomed us in, his voice carried warmth tinged with curiosity about our visit.

"Harold, we need your help," Robert said. "We're looking into some old cases, and we need any information you might have on a man named Marcus Hill."

Harold hesitated, adjusting his glasses with a skeptical look. "I'm sorry, but I can't just give out information like that. It's confidential."

I exchanged a determined glance with Robert, a silent understanding passing between us. Taking a deep breath, I reached into my purse and pulled out a thick bundle of bills. Placing it on the counter, I slid it toward Harold, my voice steady but urgent.

"Please, Harold," I implored. "We really need your help. This is important."

His eyes flickered down to the money, a brief conflict playing across his face. After a moment's hesitation, he sighed heavily, his resolve softening. "Alright, alright," he muttered, gathering the bills and stuffing them into his pocket. "I'll see what I can do."

He shuffled off to the back room and returned with a thick file. "This is everything we have on Hill. He was a strange one, always kept to himself. There were rumors, of course, but nothing ever came of them."

We thanked Harold and took the file to a nearby table, spreading out its contents. Inside were old articles, photographs, and notes. One photograph stood out — a grainy image of a man standing by the creek, his expression grim. It was Hill.

I quickly pointed to a note scrawled on the back of the photograph. "Look at this," I said. Written in hurried handwriting were the words, "He knows more than he's letting on." Robert's eyes narrowed as he studied the note. "We need to find out where Hill went. He's the key to all of this."

We spent the rest of the day chasing leads on Hill's whereabouts, each dead-end weighing heavily. But finally, we caught a break: a former neighbor recalled seeing Hill leave town with a man named Joseph Turner, a reclusive figure known to live in a cabin deep in the woods.

"Turner's a bit of a hermit," the neighbor had said, shaking his head. "Keeps to himself. If Hill's with him, it won't be easy to find them."

Determined, Robert and I prepared for a trip into the woods. As we packed supplies and mapped out the route, I couldn't shake the feeling that we were getting closer. Each clue pointed us in a direction, and I was more determined than ever to see this through.

At dawn, we set out, the woods ahead looming vast and untamed. We hiked for hours, the trail fading with each step as the forest thickened. But we pressed on, driven by hope and a quiet resolve.

As the sun began to dip below the trees, we finally spotted Turner's cabin, nearly hidden in the shadows of the dense forest. It was a small, rustic structure, barely visible through the thick undergrowth. We approached cautiously, unsure of what to expect.

With my heart pounding, I knocked on the door. After a long, tense moment, it creaked open, revealing a grizzled, unkempt man who glared at us with suspicion.

"What do you want?" Turner growled, his voice rough as gravel.

Taking a steadying breath, I replied, "We're

looking for Marcus Hill. We believe he knows something about my sister's disappearance."

A flicker of recognition passed through Turner's piercing blue eyes, but he stood unmoved. "Hill's not here," he said sharply. "Haven't seen him in years. Now get off my property. Don't waste my time with your nonsense. I've got better things to do."

Turner embodied solitude. His graying beard and weathered skin spoke of days spent battling the elements. Clad in worn, practical clothes, he looked like he'd wrestled hardship and come out harder himself. There was an undeniable command in his presence, a sharpness in his gaze that suggested he missed little, even here in isolation.

Before I could respond, Turner slammed the door, the force rattling the frame and echoing through the quiet woods, leaving us standing there in stunned silence.

My heart sank, a cold despair settling over me. With his rejection, it felt as though the last fragile shred of hope slipped through my fingers. A tear slipped down my cheek, but I wiped it away quickly, unwilling to let him — or anyone — see my despair. His dismissiveness, his cold, piercing eyes, had cut deep. I'd been holding myself together, but now, I felt on the verge of breaking.

Gripping Robert's arm, I whispered, my voice barely holding steady, "I don't know how much more of this I can take. Every lead is a dead end. Turner was our last hope."

Robert, calm and steady as always, wrapped his hand over mine, giving it a reassuring squeeze. "We'll find her, Amanda. We have to keep going."

I shook my head, unable to stop the tears now. "But look at our journey, Robert. Every single person we've met — none of them helped us out of kindness. They've either ignored us, or worse, acted like we're a nuisance. No one can see how much Clara means to me, or how much I need her back."

Turner had been listening to us from the window. As he heard my words, a softness seemed to break through his hardened demeanor. Slowly, he opened the door, his expression less guarded. "I'm not willing to help you," he began, his voice gruff but tinged with something almost vulnerable. "But hearing you... it made me reconsider. Maybe it's because I lost my own family when I was young. I understand the pain of losing someone you love."

He stepped aside and gestured for us to enter. "Come inside. Let's talk about it."

The sudden shift in his tone took me by surprise. I exchanged a hopeful glance with Robert before following Turner into the dimly lit cabin. As he closed the door behind us, the sound echoed in the confined space, almost ominously. He lit a lantern, casting a faint glow over his weathered face and the cluttered room. Dusty furniture, scattered papers, and the hunting trophies on the walls painted a picture of a man who had chosen to retreat from the world. Shadows clung to every corner, as though they, too, held secrets waiting to be unearthed.

Turner settled into a worn chair, his eyes meeting mine with newfound empathy. "Tell me everything," he said, his voice low. "Every detail about Clara, and maybe... just maybe, we'll find something that can help."

THE VANISHING POINT

As we shared our story, I felt a fragile hope ignite within me. Turner's unexpected change of heart, his willingness to listen, gave me strength. I clung to the possibility that this might be the break we so desperately needed.

When we finished, Turner began to speak, his voice a rough whisper. "There are things you don't know about this place... things that go deeper than what's on the surface. Clara's disappearance is part of something much bigger, something dangerous."

A chill crept over me as he spoke, painting a picture of secrets, betrayal, and shadows lurking behind the facade of our quiet town. His words carried weight, each one sinking into me and adding to the ache I felt for my sister. Yet, a spark of hope burned through the fear, stronger than ever before.

But despite the hope, pain gnawed at me, relentless and raw. Clara's face flashed in my mind — her smile, her laughter, our bond. The thought of never seeing her again was a darkness I could barely endure. I tightened my grip on Robert's hand, grounding myself in the determination to bring Clara home, no matter what.

Chapter 5

The Waterside Revelation

Robert and I sat across from Turner, our eyes locked on his weathered face as he began to speak. "I've been living out here for years, away from the madness of town," he said, his voice low and steady. "One day, Hill showed up, looking for a place to hide. He was scared, muttering about things that didn't make much sense at the time."

I leaned forward, my voice barely a whisper. "What things?"

Turner's gaze flickered to me, then shifted to Robert before he continued. "He talked about a group of powerful people in Silver Creek, ones who control everything from the shadows. He said they were involved in all kinds of activities—smuggling, bribery... even disappearances."

My heart raced. "Disappearances like my sister's?"

Turner gave a slow nod. "He didn't give details, but he hinted that a girl might have been taken because she knew too much or had seen something she shouldn't have."

Robert's jaw clenched, a hard resolve settling into his features. "Where's Hill now? We need to find him."

Turner shrugged, his voice trailing off as he remembered. "He stayed here for a while, then vanished. I'm not sure if he was talking about your sister, Clara, or someone else. Hill said he was close to finding proof, something that would expose this group. He mentioned that a girl could help him, but I haven't seen him since."

Rising from his chair, Turner moved to a pile of old boxes in the corner, rummaging through them until he pulled out a worn leather journal. "This was his. Maybe it'll have something that can help you."

I took the journal, feeling a strange connection

to this elusive man. As I opened it, the pages revealed an obsessive documentation of names, dates, and places—a roadmap of Hill's journey to expose the truth. But it was the last entry that caught my eye.

"They're onto me. If I disappear, it means they've found me. But I've hidden something they'll never find. The key is in the place where the water meets the stone."

I showed the note to Robert and asked, "What does that mean?"

He frowned. "It's cryptic, but it sounds like a clue. We need to figure out where 'the place where the water meets the stone' is."

Turner sighed. "There's a place like that near the old quarry, just outside of town. People used to go there to fish, but it's been abandoned for years."

Robert nodded. "Then that's where we'll start. Thank you, Mr. Turner. You've been a big help."

As we left the cabin and headed back through the woods, the setting sun cast long shadows across our path. Hill's urgent words hung over us, driving us forward.

As Robert drove us back to town, questions swirled in my mind like a turbulent whirlpool. I turned to him, my voice tinged with desperation and anxiety.

"Why would Clara willingly go into the forest at night if she was kidnapped? Is she even alive?" The questions spilled out in rapid succession, each one a dagger of uncertainty.

Robert's brow furrowed in deep thought, his eyes fixed on the road ahead. "Amanda, we can't be certain she was kidnapped. There's so much we don't understand yet."

"But why would someone be after Clara?" I persisted, frustration seeping into my voice. "She was innocent, Robert. Innocent!"

Robert sighed heavily, his voice laced with concern. "Enemies aren't always born, Amanda. Sometimes, circumstances create them. Maybe Clara stumbled upon something, something she wasn't meant to know."

His words struck a nerve. "But she was always cautious, Robert. She wouldn't have put herself in harm's way willingly," I insisted, my voice betraying

THE VANISHING POINT

the fear gripping my heart.

Robert nodded slowly, his expression grave. "You're right. Clara was careful. But sometimes, even the most cautious people find themselves in dangerous situations."

As we approached my house, Robert redirected the conversation, shifting focus to the ominous notes we'd been receiving.

"The notes are troubling," I admitted, unease coloring my voice. "Someone is watching us, observing our every move."

"And what's strange is that these warnings only started again after so long," I continued, my mind racing with possibilities. "Why now, after all this time?"

Robert furrowed his brow, deep in thought. "It's a mystery, Amanda. But before we confront Hill, we need to find some answers ourselves. You know Clara better than anyone; you might hold the key to understanding all of this."

Back at my house, we settled in, the weight of uncertainty pressing down on us like a heavy blanket.

Robert turned to me, his eyes searching mine with a mixture of concern and determination.

"Amanda, think carefully," he began, his voice gentle yet insistent. "Is there anything about Clara — any connections, any incidents — that might explain why she's in danger?"

I closed my eyes, searching my memory for any clue that could unravel the mystery. Suddenly, a memory surfaced, sending a chill down my spine. "There was an incident with our stepmother," I began slowly, the words spilling out in a rush. "When my mother became very ill, our father had just remarried a woman from our neighborhood — Aunt Angela, a widow. She moved in with her son, Kevin.

"Clara struggled to accept it. She couldn't understand how our father could marry someone else while our mother was still sick. She became very upset and started to resent our father, Aunt Angela, and even Kevin."

Aunt Angela was a tall, elegant woman with an air of sophistication that often seemed out of place in our small town. Her perfectly styled auburn hair and meticulously chosen outfits made her stand out wherever she went. She carried herself with a certain aloofness, and her piercing green eyes seemed to assess everything and everyone critically. Though she tried to be kind, there was a coldness in her demeanor that made it difficult for Clara to accept her.

Kevin, on the other hand, was a clever and mischievous boy. His sandy blond hair and constant grin hinted at his playful nature. He had a knack for getting into trouble and seemed to delight in teasing Clara whenever he could. From hiding her belongings to playing pranks, Kevin's antics only deepened Clara's resentment. His quick wit often got him out of tight spots, making him a constant source of irritation for her as he navigated the new family dynamics with a devilish charm.

Clara and Kevin didn't get along at all. They argued incessantly, blaming each other for everything that went wrong. The house was filled with their shouting and accusations, turning an already difficult time into something almost unbearable for us all.

After our mother passed away, the house felt

emptier than ever. Grief hung in the air, heavy and suffocating. My father tried to keep things together, but the pain of losing her was overwhelming.

Clara's anger only grew. She couldn't forgive our father for remarrying so soon, and her resentment toward Aunt Angela and Kevin intensified. Every interaction with Kevin turned into a shouting match; they blamed each other for the smallest things, from missing school supplies to chores left undone.

The constant fighting made it impossible to find any peace. Our mother's loss had left a wound in our family, and the new dynamics only deepened it. It felt as though we were all trapped in a storm, struggling to find our way back to calmer waters.

"And after a year, Aunt Angela passed away. It was cancer—terminal stage. But our stepbrother Kevin accused us of foul play. He believed we were responsible for her death."

Robert's expression hardened. "Your stepbrother—does he still hold a grudge against Clara?"

I shook my head firmly. "No, Robert. He

couldn't have... he was just a teenager then, and he had no means to harm anyone. Besides, it was proven that our stepmother's death was from natural causes."

One evening, Clara and I stepped out into the cool air, feeling a mix of sadness and relief. We walked down the street, the weight of the past few months slowly lifting from our shoulders. It was time to find a new place to call home, somewhere we could begin to heal and move forward.

Robert asked where we lived after leaving our house. I told him I preferred the orphanage because I couldn't continue living in a place filled with so much pain and conflict.

He encouraged me to share more about it. I took a deep breath, gathering my thoughts.

"After everything with Clara, I needed a fresh start. One of my professors mentioned an orphanage just beyond the outskirts of Silver Creek, and several friends spoke highly of it. They said it was a place where I could find peace."

There, we met Miss Olivia, the owner of the orphanage, who welcomed us with open arms. It felt like a chance to escape our past and begin to heal. Soon, Miss Olivia and the children became our new family.

Miss Olivia was a graceful woman with soft, silver hair that cascaded in gentle waves down her shoulders. Her warm brown eyes were framed by delicate laugh lines, reflecting a kindness that radiated from her every gesture. She had a gentle demeanor and was often seen wearing cozy, pastel-colored sweaters that complemented her serene presence. Her genuine smile had a way of putting others at ease, and her soothing voice conveyed deep empathy and understanding.

Robert pondered my words for a moment, then spoke thoughtfully. "Then why did you move here if you were both happily living there?"

"Robert, when I turned eighteen, I knew we couldn't stay at the orphanage forever. I had to think about Clara's future, especially her education. Then, one day, I received a job offer back in Silver Creek. It wasn't just any job — it came with housing and a decent salary. It was a fresh start I couldn't pass up."

"That sounds like a great opportunity," Robert

remarked. "But what about Clara? How did she feel about moving back here?"

"Clara was about to start university," I explained, "and the university she wanted to attend was right here in Silver Creek. It felt like everything was falling into place. She was excited about her studies, and I was relieved we could stay together."

Robert leaned back, taking it all in. "It sounds like you made the right decision. You both have done well for yourselves."

Pride filled my chest, and I smiled. "Yes, it wasn't always easy, but we made it work. This neighborhood has become our home, and we've built a life here."

"How long have you been in this house now?" Robert asked.

"Just six or seven years," I replied. "In that time, we've made so many friends and feel like we're part of several families."

"Did Clara have anyone special?" Robert asked, leaning in. "It might give us a clue about her disappearance."

I shook my head slowly. "No, I don't think anyone here was involved in Clara going missing. We had such a wonderful time in this neighborhood. Everyone loved Clara and me. One family, in particular, was very close to us — Miss Janiya's family."

"Clara's best friend was Mona, Miss Janiya's daughter."

Robert's eyes lit up with a hint of hope. "Maybe Mona or Miss Janiya knows something we don't."

"No," I replied firmly. "They don't. Before Clara disappeared, she spent most of her time with Mona. Mona and her family were devastated when Clara went missing. It was a shock to everyone. We investigated, but nothing turned up. It was as if she vanished without a trace."

Robert's face softened. "We still have hope. Maybe soon, we'll find out what happened to her."

I sighed, feeling the weight of uncertainty pressing down on me. "I don't know, Robert. All we need now is evidence."

"Tomorrow, we'll find Hill," Robert declared with determination.

"Of course, but right now, you need rest."

I nodded, grateful for Robert's steadfast presence amidst the turmoil. "Thank you, Robert. I don't know what I'd do without you."

"We'll find Clara, Amanda," he reassured me, his voice unwavering. "No matter what it takes." With that, he headed back to his house. But sleep eluded me as questions haunted me, echoing in the silence of the night.

The next morning, we set out for the old quarry. It was a desolate place, filled with rusting machinery and piles of rubble. The water was still and dark, mirroring the grey sky above. As we walked along the edge, a sense of unease crept over me, as though we were being watched.

We reached a spot where a large boulder jutted out into the water. "This must be it," Robert said. "The place where the water meets the stone."

We searched the area, combing through every crevice. After what felt like hours, I spotted a small metal box wedged in a rock crevice. My hands shook as I pulled it out and opened it.

Inside was a bundle of papers and a flash drive. The papers were filled with notes and diagrams detailing the activities of a secret group Hill had mentioned. The flash drive, I hoped, would reveal even more.

I said "We need to get this back to the library. We need to see what's on this drive."

Back at the library, we plugged the flash drive into my computer and opened the files. They contained a trove of information—emails, financial records, and photographs. Hill had been right. A powerful group in Silver Creek had been operating in the shadows for years, covering their tracks and silencing anyone who got too close to the truth.

One email, in particular, caught my attention. It was a correspondence between two members of the group, discussing the need to silence a "nosy girl" who had seen too much. The date matched the time of Clara's disappearance.

"This is it," I whispered, my voice trembling. "This is the proof we need."

Robert's eyes darkened with determination. "We need to take this to the authorities, but we have to be careful. These people are dangerous."

Just as we prepared to leave, my phone buzzed with a message from an unknown number: "You're getting too close. Back off now, or you'll regret it."

I showed the message to Robert, who frowned. "They know we're onto them. We need to move fast."

With the evidence in hand, we headed to the sheriff's office. But as we approached, a black SUV pulled up alongside us. Men in suits stepped out, their expressions cold and menacing.

"You need to come with us," one of them said, his tone leaving no room for argument.

Robert stepped in front of me, his hand resting on his gun. "We're not going anywhere with you."

The man smirked. "You don't have a choice."

Before I could react, they grabbed us, forcing us into the SUV. As the vehicle sped away, I realized just how deep and dangerous this conspiracy went. But I also knew I wouldn't stop until I found Clara and brought these people to justice.

The darkness around us seemed to close in, yet a spark of hope remained. We had the evidence. Now, we just needed to survive long enough to use it. The battle was far from over, and the stakes had never been higher.

The SUV's interior was shrouded in darkness, the tinted windows blocking any glimpse of the outside. The men who had taken us sat in silent vigilance, their faces impassive and cold. Robert and I exchanged a glance, both of us wordlessly gauging our options. My heart thundered, but I focused on keeping my fear in check.

The drive felt endless. The SUV wound through twisting roads and sharp turns, leaving me disoriented and tense. Finally, we pulled up in front of an abandoned warehouse on the outskirts of Silver Creek. The building loomed like a forgotten giant, its shattered windows and graffiti-streaked walls radiating menace.

"Out," one of the men ordered, pulling me roughly from the SUV. Robert followed, his eyes blazing with anger and defiance. We were led inside, the dim light filtering through broken windows casting eerie shadows across the walls. They shoved us into a small room, empty except for a metal table and a few chairs, binding our hands behind our backs as we sat.

The door creaked open, and a man entered. Tall and imposing, he radiated authority, his cold, calculating gaze piercing through us. A cruel smile flickered on his lips as he sized us up.

"Welcome," he said, his voice smooth yet mocking. "I'm surprised you've made it this far."

"Who are you?" I demanded, injecting my voice with a courage I barely felt.

He chuckled. "My name is irrelevant. What matters is that you've stumbled into things you shouldn't have."

"We know what you're doing," Robert shot back, his voice steady and firm. "And we have evidence. You can't keep this hidden forever."

The man's smile vanished. "You're mistaken if you think anyone will believe you. We've controlled Silver Creek for years. We own the police, the officials — everyone."

"We'll see about that," I retorted.

His eyes narrowed, the glint in them growing colder. "You're very brave, Ms. Crater. It's a shame it won't do you any good."

With that, he turned and left, the door slamming behind him. Silence filled the room, heavy and foreboding as the reality of our situation closed in around us.

"Robert," I whispered urgently, "we have to get out of here."

He nodded, his eyes scanning the room, searching for anything that could offer us a way out. "Stay calm. We'll figure something out."

Time dragged on, each minute sharpening the dread that gnawed at me. I tried to concentrate on breathing, pushing the fear back down. Suddenly, the door burst open, and one of the guards rushed in, clearly agitated.

"We have to move them. Now," he barked at the others.

Without explanation, they untied us and pulled

us from the chairs, giving us no chance to resist. As we stumbled through the darkened hallways of the warehouse, I noticed a door slightly ajar. It was a slim chance—but right now, it was our only chance.

As we passed through the door, I stumbled, causing the guard holding me to lose his grip. Seizing the moment, I shoved him away and bolted through the opening. Robert was right behind me, and together, we sprinted down a narrow corridor, the shouts of our captors echoing behind us.

We burst into the open air, the evening light blinding us after the dimness of the warehouse. We didn't stop, racing toward the woods that bordered the area. The sound of footsteps and shouting grew louder as our pursuers gained on us.

My lungs burned, and my legs felt like lead, but I forced myself to keep going. Robert grabbed my hand, pulling me along when I started to slow. We weaved through the trees, the dense foliage providing some cover.

Eventually, the sounds of pursuit faded, and we slowed to a walk, both of us gasping for breath. We kept moving, not daring to stop until we were sure we had lost them.

"Where to now?" I asked, my voice barely more than a gasp.

"We need to find a place to lay low and go through the evidence—somewhere they won't think to look," Robert replied.

We made our way to an old hunting cabin deep in the woods, one that Robert's family had owned for years but rarely used. It was small and dusty, but it provided shelter and, more importantly, safety.

As night fell, we huddled around a small lamp, sifting through the documents and files we'd retrieved. The information was damning, revealing that this group had its hands in everything—from local businesses to law enforcement. We could barely comprehend the extent of their reach, the depth of their influence.

"We need to find out what they're hiding," Robert said, breaking the silence. "The activities they're involved in, who's behind it all, and what Clara's link is to this." His voice was steady, but an undercurrent of urgency and determination ran through it.

"Yes," I replied. "We need to uncover who's pulling the strings." As we continued delving into the documents, a sense of foreboding settled over us. But we were determined to find the truth, no matter the cost.

Chapter 6

Confronting Hill

The drive to Hill's last known location was tense, each mile bringing us closer to the truth—and to the potential danger that awaited us. Robert's expression was unreadable, his focus fixed on the road as I sat beside him, gripping the worn leather journal Hill had left behind.

We had just turned onto a less-traveled road when Robert's phone rang, breaking the silence. He glanced at the caller ID, then at me, his expression shifting to cautious optimism. "It's Turner," he said, answering the call.

"Hey, Robert," Turner's voice came through the speaker, filled with a mix of excitement and relief. "I've got good news for you."

Robert's eyes sharpened as he listened. "What's the update?"

"I managed to track down Hill's current location," Turner said. "I used some of the surveillance footage we retrieved from the area where he was last seen. We picked up a few distinctive features that matched his movements."

I watched Robert's expression shift from tension to cautious hope. "Where is he?"

Turner's voice was steady and confident. "He's holed up in an old warehouse on the outskirts of town. It's a bit rundown and hidden from the main roads, which explains why it took us a while to locate him. The place is surrounded by dense forest, making it a perfect hideout."

Robert relayed the information to me, his grip on the steering wheel tightening. "We're heading there now. Any other details we should know?"

Turner's tone grew more serious. "Be careful. The place has been abandoned for a while, but it looks like Hill might have set up some makeshift security. There's also a possibility he's not alone. It's crucial you approach with caution."

"Got it," Robert said, ending the call. He turned to me, his face a mix of determination and concern.

"We've got our lead. We need to move quickly."

As we drove toward the warehouse, the tension was palpable. The familiar sights of Silver Creek faded, replaced by an increasingly desolate landscape. Hill's whereabouts were finally within reach, but the danger was far from over.

We arrived at the warehouse, its exterior just as Turner had described — dilapidated and partially obscured by overgrown vegetation. The building looked abandoned, but a sense of foreboding hung in the air, suggesting it was anything but deserted.

Robert parked the car a short distance away, and we approached on foot. The quiet was unsettling; the only sound was the crunch of leaves beneath our feet. Hill was inside, and we had to be ready for anything.

We stepped into the warehouse, the cold, musty air heavy around us. Hill was in an old storage room, his eyes flicking toward us as we entered, a mixture of fear and resignation etched on his face.

He was a wiry man in his early forties, with unkempt hair that hadn't seen a barber in months. His clothes—a worn-out jacket and faded jeans—were a stark contrast to the high-stakes situation he now faced. His face was gaunt, marked by a scruffy beard and eyes that darted nervously around the room. He fidgeted with the frayed edge of his jacket, struggling to maintain a facade of bravado. When he spoke, his voice was strained, a mix of defensiveness and desperation, as though he was on the brink of panic but trying to hold it together.

"Sit down, Hill," Robert ordered, his tone firm. Hill complied, sinking into a rickety chair. Robert sat across from him, his gaze steady and unyielding.

Hill's eyes widened as he took in our presence. "Who are you?" Hill demanded. "How did you get in here? This is private property. I should call security!"

Before he could make a move, Robert swiftly crossed the room, clamping a hand over Hill's mouth to silence him. "Don't even think about it," Robert said, his voice low and dangerous. "We're not here to play games."

I stepped forward, pulling out the evidence we had gathered—the documents and photographs linking him to various illegal activities. I placed them on the table between us, ensuring Hill had a clear view.

Robert's gaze was unyielding. "If we don't hear from our friend within half an hour or if we don't leave this place by then, the police will be here. You're not in a position to refuse our help. We know you're involved in some serious crimes, but that's not our concern right now. We just need information—nothing more, nothing less."

Hill's face paled as he absorbed the evidence, his eyes darting nervously between us and the incriminating documents. "You don't understand," he said, his voice trembling. "I was deceived. I thought I was working with someone on the right side, but I've been played. I've lost everything because of this."

Robert's expression softened slightly, though his tone remained firm. "What do you mean? What's your connection to all of this?"

Hill slumped in his chair, his shoulders shaking

slightly. "I'm not just a participant. I'm a victim too. My daughter Emily — she's missing. I don't even know if she's alive. I've been hiding out here, trying to keep my other children safe from these cruel people. They're powerful and merciless."

A pang of sympathy hit me as I saw the desperation in his eyes. "Then help us," I urged. "Tell us everything you know. We need to find out what's really going on and who's behind all of this."

Hill looked up at us, a mixture of fear and resolve filling his gaze. "I'll help you. I've been trying to escape from these people for a long time. They've kept me in the dark, but I know the location they're operating from. It's hidden away, and I can take you there."

Robert nodded, his expression resolute. "Lead the way. But remember, if you're lying to us or if you try to run, we'll have no choice but to turn everything over to the authorities."

Hill nodded slowly, his face a mask of regret and determination. We left the warehouse and followed him into the woods, the path winding and overgrown. As we walked, the eerie familiarity of the surroundings gnawed at my memory, but I couldn't place why this place felt so significant.

The journey through the forest felt interminable, each step bringing us closer to a truth that seemed just out of reach. Hill's directions led us to a clearing, and as we emerged into the open, I gasped. The scene before me was hauntingly familiar. The old building in the clearing looked almost exactly like the one in the photograph I had seen earlier, but the specifics eluded me.

Noticing my distress, Robert placed a reassuring hand on my shoulder. "Amanda, what is it? Do you recognize this place?"

"I don't know," I replied, frustration evident in my voice. "I've been here before, but I can't remember why."

Hill's face flickered with concern. "If you've been here before, it means they might have anticipated your search."

My mind raced, trying to connect the pieces of my past with the present reality. The clearing and the old building were unmistakably linked to something I had experienced, but the details remained just out of reach.

Robert's focus shifted back to the task at hand. "We need to search this place thoroughly. There might be something here that can help us understand what's really going on."

As we began our search, the sense of urgency grew. The connection between Hill's past, my own memories, and the criminal activities was becoming clearer, yet the full picture remained shrouded in darkness. The weight of our discoveries felt heavy, and with each passing moment, the danger seemed to close in around us.

I sat beneath a large oak tree, its leaves rustling softly in the breeze. This place was disconcertingly familiar, yet elusive, like a half-remembered dream. The old building and the overgrown grounds stirred something deep within me, but my memory refused to fully cooperate. Every detail lingered on the edge of recognition, just out of reach.

The confusion was overwhelming. I tried to

focus, but the more I thought, the more the memories slipped away. I was so lost in my thoughts that I barely noticed Robert approaching until he gently placed a hand on my shoulder.

"Amanda, are you okay?" His voice was tinged with concern.

I looked up at him, feeling a mix of frustration and vulnerability. "I'm not sure, Robert. This place... it feels so familiar, but I can't place why. It's like I've been here before, but I can't remember any specifics."

Robert crouched down beside me, his expression earnest. "This might be an important clue, Amanda. If this place is linked to something you've experienced, it could help us understand what's really going on. Try to focus on your memories. Anything might be relevant."

I nodded, taking a deep breath to steady my racing thoughts. I reached into my bag and pulled out my cellphone, hoping a visual prompt might jog my memory. I opened my old photo gallery and began scrolling through the images.

My thumb hesitated over one photograph, a

snapshot from a summer vacation years ago. The image showed a quaint farmhouse, surrounded by lush greenery. My heart skipped a beat as I realized that the farmhouse in the photograph looked strikingly similar to the one before me. It was an old, rustic building with a charm that felt oddly comforting and unsettling at the same time.

"Wait, wait," I said aloud, my voice catching with excitement. "This place... it's like the one Miss Olivia and her husband have near Silver Creek. We visited them during summer vacation years ago when we were part of that orphanage. It's about six hours from Silver Creek, but it's remarkably similar."

Robert leaned closer, clearly intrigued. "Miss Olivia? The same Miss Olivia who owned the orphanage?"

"Yes," I confirmed, my voice growing more confident. "Her husband's hospital looks similar to that place," I said, pointing to the building behind us. "It's a sanctuary where patients are treated with care, just like the facility here. I remember that Miss Olivia used to speak about her husband's hospital often."

Robert's eyes lit up with realization. "That's a crucial connection. If this place resembles that hospital and is linked to her, it could be central to understanding the crimes we're investigating. But you mentioned something about an orphanage?"

I nodded, feeling a sense of urgency. "Yes, Miss Olivia is associated with a well-known orphanage, and her husband owned that hospital, which looks like the building we're standing in front of."

Robert's expression grew serious. "That's valuable information. We should investigate further to confirm if there's a direct link between this place and that hospital. If Miss Olivia's involvement extends beyond what we know, it could uncover more about the motives behind the crimes."

I stood up, feeling a renewed sense of purpose. "Yes, we need to explore this place. If Miss Olivia is involved in something bigger, we need to understand her role and how it ties into the larger picture. This could be the key to solving the mystery."

With Hill's help, we managed to get inside the facility, which was in such a rough state that no one would suspect anyone could live there. The exterior was weathered, with broken windows and overgrown ivy giving it an abandoned look. Once inside, we carefully investigated the first floor, ensuring we remained unrecognizable. The rooms appeared to have once been part of a hospital, now filled with old furniture and dusty patient records. Despite our thorough search, we found nothing unusual or noteworthy.

We decided to move to the second floor. As we ascended, we encountered a janitor. We explained that we were researchers studying old, damaged buildings. Initially, he refused to let us proceed, but after we slipped him some cash, he reluctantly agreed. He warned us that we had only one day because the staff was on leave and had gone home. He also cautioned us not to delve too deeply, as the owner often checked the building. With that, he departed with some other maintenance staff for lunch.

We continued our search on the second floor but found nothing special. The rooms were similar to those on the first floor, filled with old furniture and patient records. Frustration began to set in as we realized our efforts might be in vain. We were about to leave when we started blaming Hill for misleading us. It seemed like nothing more than an old hospital.

However, Hill insisted he was informed about this location and had received calls from here years ago. Despite our initial disappointment, we decided to give Hill the benefit of the doubt. We regrouped and planned our next steps, realizing there was still a chance this building held the key to understanding Miss Olivia's broader network of charitable work and her potential involvement in the crimes.

The old building had an eerie stillness, with every creak and groan of the ancient structure echoing through its hollow corridors. The smell of mildew and decay permeated the air, a testament to the many years it had stood neglected. As we made our way back down to the first floor, we paused to reassess our approach. Hill, ever the optimist, suggested we check the basement. Reluctantly, we agreed, though the thought of descending into the dark, musty underbelly of the building filled us with dread.

The entrance to the basement was concealed behind a heavy, rusted door at the end of a narrow hallway. With considerable effort, we managed to pry it open, the metal hinges protesting loudly. A steep staircase led down into the pitch-black darkness below. Armed with only our flashlights, we began our descent, each step echoing ominously in the confined space.

The basement was even more decrepit than the floors above. The air was thick with dust, and the walls were lined with cobwebs. Broken equipment and discarded furniture were strewn about haphazardly, creating an obstacle course of sorts. We split up, each of us taking a different section of the basement to search. The oppressive silence was broken only by the occasional scurrying of rats and the distant sound of dripping water.

Despite the uninviting environment, we pressed on, determined to find some clue that would justify our efforts. It was Hill who first noticed the false wall. He called us over, and together we examined the area more closely. The wall was constructed of newer materials, incongruent with the rest of the basement's aged and crumbling structure. With a mixture of excitement and apprehension, we set to work dismantling it.

Behind the false wall, we discovered a hidden room. It was small and cramped, offering just enough space to move around. The room contained a few pieces of furniture: a rickety table, a couple of chairs, and a dusty filing cabinet. But what caught our attention were the stacks of documents piled haphazardly around the room. These were no ordinary patient records; they were detailed files on various individuals, complete with personal information, financial records, and even surveillance photos.

The significance of our discovery hit us like a freight train. These files were evidence of something much larger and more sinister than we had anticipated. Hill's contact had been right; this building was not just an abandoned hospital but a hub of clandestine activity. As we sifted through the documents, a clearer picture began to emerge. The names listed in the files were all connected to Miss

Olivia's charitable organization, but the information suggested they were involved in illegal activities.

The realization struck us hard. Miss Olivia, a respected philanthropist known for her charitable works, was at the center of a criminal network. As we examined the documents, we found a reference to a farmhouse near a forest on the outskirts of the city. It seemed to be the next clue in our investigation, and we knew we had to follow it. However, we had to proceed with caution. Our discovery put us in a precarious position; if Miss Olivia or her associates learned of our investigation, our lives could be in danger.

We decided to take as many documents as we could carry and swiftly exited the building. We carefully replaced the false wall to hide our intrusion. As we made our way back to the surface, the gravity of our situation settled in. We needed to contact the authorities, but we had to do so in a way that would ensure our safety and preserve the integrity of the evidence.

Outside, the afternoon sun began to set, casting long shadows across the dilapidated building. We moved quickly and quietly, not wanting to attract attention. Once we were a safe distance away, we regrouped and formulated a plan. Our next step was to explore that farmhouse.

Chapter 7

Veil of Secrets

We decided to approach the farmhouse with extreme caution. Robert insisted that the main roads were too dangerous; tracking our movements would be all too easy. He proposed we take a shortcut along a hidden path to ensure our safety.

We approached a nearby neighbor, an elderly man who appeared surprisingly sharp for his age. After offering him some money, we asked if he knew of any concealed routes to the farmhouse. Initially, he was hesitant, wary of our intentions and the potential risks involved. However, after some persuasion, he agreed to guide us, revealing a shortcut that would keep us out of sight.

As we prepared to leave, Robert turned to Hill.

"You can go back now. It might be more dangerous ahead."

Hill's face was set with determination as he shook his head. "No. I need to stay with you. My daughter's disappearance weighs on me just as much as Amanda's sister does on her."

Robert nodded, respecting Hill's resolve. We climbed into the car—Robert at the wheel, me in the passenger seat, and Hill in the back. The tension was palpable as we navigated the dense forest, relying on the old man's directions.

Curiosity gnawed at me, and I turned to Hill. "Did you know about Clara's disappearance beforehand?"

He shook his head, his expression somber. "No, I didn't. I was only informed by one of the group's members that a girl was causing trouble and posing a danger to us. They wanted to 'deal' with her. I had no idea whether they were talking about Clara or not."

I frowned, trying to piece it all together. "How was Clara involved in all this? It doesn't make sense. I wasn't even aware of any of her intentions that could lead her into danger."

Hill sighed heavily, the weight of his past evident in his voice. "I really don't know about Clara. If I had known the people I was working with were involved in such horrific activities, I would never have joined them. I took the job to support my family. I was unemployed and desperate for money. But as time went on, I realized it was all a web of evil."

Robert's curiosity piqued. "When did you first realize it was bad? Was there a particular moment that made you understand how deep it went?"

Hill's eyes grew distant as he recalled his past. "It wasn't one specific moment; it gradually became clear. I started seeing the dark side of the operations, and the more I witnessed, the more I realized I was trapped in something monstrous. I tried to get out, but then my daughter disappeared."

He paused, anguish etched on his face. "I couldn't tell anyone. I was terrified for my safety and for my family. I thought if I spoke out, it would only make things worse. I hoped she'd come back on her own, but nothing changed."

Robert's voice softened, yet urgency lingered. "So, you ended up escaping and hiding. How did you manage to get away? And why didn't you come forward sooner?"

Hill's gaze fell to the floor. "I had to keep my family safe, so I fled and went into hiding. The fear was all-consuming; I was always looking over my shoulder. It's been a life filled with regret and guilt.

Robert glanced at Hill through the rearview mirror, empathy shining in his eyes. "We'll find your daughter. Don't worry."

I listened intently to their conversation, feeling a spark of hope. "We'll find both Clara and Emily. We'll get to the bottom of this."

After what felt like hours navigating the dense forest, we finally neared the farmhouse, nestled deep within the woods, hidden from view. Robert parked the car far from the farmhouse, ensuring it was well-concealed among the trees and thick underbrush.

As we exited the vehicle, the forest around us felt eerily silent, broken only by the occasional rustle of leaves. The farmhouse stood in the distance, old and abandoned, yet an ominous aura suggested that something sinister lay within.

"We need to approach quietly," Robert whispered, leading the way. We moved cautiously, each step deliberate to avoid noise. The path was narrow, overgrown with wild plants and bushes, but we pressed on, guided by the old man who had shown us the way.

As we drew closer, the farmhouse loomed larger, its weathered exterior partially covered in ivy and moss. We finally reached the edge of the clearing surrounding the structure. Robert motioned for us to stop and crouch behind a thick cluster of bushes. He surveyed the area, his eyes scanning for any signs of movement or security.

"I don't see anyone, but we need to be careful," he instructed softly. Then he turned to Hill. "Do you know if there's anyone inside? Have you visited this place before?"

Hill shook his head. "I'm not sure. No, I haven't been here before. They might have left someone to guard the place

As we approached the front door, Robert raised a hand, signaling for us to stop. Suddenly, a noise shattered the silence—a guard stepped out from the shadows. Before we could react, he spotted us, his eyes widening in surprise.

Without hesitation, Robert lunged at the guard, grappling with him. Hill quickly joined in, helping Robert subdue the man. The struggle was brief but intense, with the guard putting up a fight. However, Robert's training and Hill's desperation gave them the upper hand. Together, they managed to tie the guard up with some rope Hill had brought along.

Robert muttered, wiping sweat from his brow, "That was close. We need to be more careful. There could be more of them."

He turned to me with urgency. "Stay here for a moment. I'll be back."

With quick, deliberate movements, he dragged the guard into the shadowed corner of the alley. The guard lay motionless, and Robert wasted no time. He swiftly changed into the unconscious man's clothes, swapping his attire for the guard's uniform. The transformation was seamless; soon, Robert was clad in the guard's outfit, complete with a hat and badge. Once he had finished, Robert adjusted the uniform, ensuring it looked convincing. He then signaled for us to follow. With his disguise, our chances of avoiding detection improved, but the road ahead remained fraught with uncertainty.

With the guard securely tied, Robert opened the farmhouse door. The inside was dark and musty, the air thick with the scent of decay. We stepped inside, the floorboards creaking under our weight. The interior matched the exterior's dilapidation, filled with broken furniture and peeling wallpaper. We moved cautiously, our flashlights cutting through the darkness.

We searched meticulously, examining every corner and crevice. Our efforts finally paid off when Hill pointed toward a door at the far end of the hallway. "That leads to the storeroom. If there's anything important, it's likely in there."

We nodded and made our way toward the door, our steps echoing in the silence. As we reached the storeroom, the door creaked open, revealing a cluttered space filled with old equipment and boxes. Despite its disarray, it was clear this room held more than just forgotten items.

We spread out, searching for clues. Robert soon discovered a hidden compartment behind a stack of old crates. He shone his flashlight on the compartment, illuminating its outline. With a final push, he pried open the concealed door.

Inside, the air was cool and musty, a welcome contrast to the oppressive heat outside. The small room was dimly lit by our flashlights, filled with the smell of decay. The walls were lined with shelves holding dusty boxes and old furniture.

We searched the area thoroughly, but just as we were about to leave, a faint sound from deeper within caught our attention. We turned and noticed a heavy steel door, slightly ajar and nearly obscured by crates.

Robert stepped forward, examining the door with a practiced eye. He noted the lock—a standard mechanism, but still secure. With a nod of determination, he turned to me and asked, "Do you have a bobby pin?"

I handed him one, and with skilled hands, he knelt by the lock and began to work with the pin. However, after several frustrating minutes, it became clear that his usual finesse wasn't enough; the lock resisted every attempt.

"Seems like we need a different approach," Robert said, frustration evident in his voice.

We stepped back to regroup. Robert scanned the room, and his eyes landed on a nearby tool kit we had overlooked. Quickly, he retrieved a few basic tools and began improvising. With a combination of tension and skill, he finally managed to force the lock open.

As the door creaked slowly, anticipation surged within us. We pushed it open further, revealing a dark, foreboding room. Our flashlights cut through the gloom, illuminating a grimy, neglected space. A shiver coursed through me as we stepped inside. The walls were lined with crude drawings and scrawled messages, hinting at the horrors that had occurred there.

My heart pounded in my chest as I peered into

the dimly lit room. In the corner, curled up and trembling, was a young girl. Her wide, terrified eyes darted around the room as she clutched a frayed blanket tightly around her. It was clear she had endured an incredibly distressing experience.

The girl looked up at us, a mix of fear and hope flickering in her gaze. "Daddy?" she whispered, her voice trembling.

Hill's reaction was immediate and heart-wrenching. His eyes widened in disbelief and agony at the sight of her. A pained gasp escaped his lips, and he stumbled forward, each step heavy with desperation.

"That's my daughter Emily!" he cried out, his voice soft but filled with emotion. His words were a raw, visceral outcry, a mix of shock, sorrow, and fierce love. Tears streamed down his face as he reached out, his hands shaking uncontrollably.

Emily's eyes, once filled with fear, softened at the sight of her father. She reached for him, her small frame quivering with a mixture of relief and residual terror. Hill's trembling hands gently cradled her, and for a moment, the harsh reality of their situation seemed to dissolve into a tender emotional reunion.

Hill wrapped his arms around Emily, holding her close as if he could erase the pain of their separation with his embrace. He buried his face in her hair, his sobs muffled against her tiny form. The anguish in his eyes starkly contrasted with the fragile hope reflected in Emily's gaze.

"I thought I'd lost you forever," Hill whispered brokenly, his voice choked with emotion. Emily clung to him tightly, her tears mingling with his.

Emily was a frail-looking girl, her long, dark hair tangled and unkempt, cascading over her shoulders. Her pale skin was marred by bruises and dirt, highlighting the severity of her recent experiences. She wore a simple, worn dress that hung loosely on her thin frame. Despite her disheveled appearance, there was resilience in her eyes—a glimmer of hope that hadn't been extinguished by her suffering. The sight of her clinging to the blanket for comfort and protection was both heart-wrenching and uplifting, a stark reminder of the stakes they were dealing with.

Before we left, we asked Emily if she had seen Clara. Emily shook her head and said, "No, there's nothing else here but me. Let's get out of here. I know everything—I'll tell you. This place has nothing, just dangers.

As we prepared to leave, the sound of footsteps echoed in the hallways outside. My pulse quickened as Robert signaled for us to move quickly. We had to escape before anyone discovered us.

Robert and I helped Emily and Hill navigate the dark passageways, our movements swift and cautious. Every sound seemed amplified, and every shadow felt like a potential threat. The fear of being caught added urgency to our escape.

We finally emerged from the hidden compartment, our hearts pounding. The farmhouse's main area was eerily quiet, but we couldn't take any risks, so we led the way back through the house, moving with purpose and avoiding unnecessary noise.

As we reached the exterior of the farmhouse, Robert checked for any signs of trouble. The coast seemed clear, but the danger was far from over. We made our way back through the dense forest, our steps quick but careful.

Once we reached the car, Hill's daughter was safely settled inside, wrapped in a blanket for warmth. Hill was by her side, his relief and gratitude palpable. The ordeal had taken a toll on all of us, but the sight of Emily's safe return was a powerful reminder of why we had persevered.

Robert drove us back to his farmhouse, the journey feeling both surreal and gratifying. The night was calm, a stark contrast to the chaos we had just endured. As we arrived, we could finally breathe a sigh of relief. Hill's gratitude was evident as he held his daughter close, his eyes filled with a mix of tears and joy.

The rescue had succeeded, but the threats were far from gone. We still had a lot to uncover and many questions to answer. For now, we allowed ourselves a moment of respite. The immediate danger had passed, and Emily was safe.

When we reached our place, Robert asked Hill to take Emily to her room so she could get some much-needed rest. He instructed gently, "Let her take a shower, give her something to eat, and let her get some sleep." Hill nodded, his eyes still red from the emotional reunion, and guided Emily toward a quieter part of the farmhouse.

As Emily and Hill disappeared down the hallway, I retreated to a quiet corner, overwhelmed by my emotions. I was happy to see Emily, but a deep ache lingered in my heart. I wished we had found Clara, too. The darkness seemed to swallow my frustration as I sat there, blaming God for not giving us more answers, for not letting us find Clara.

Robert approached quietly and placed a reassuring hand on my shoulder. "We did all we could," his voice steady despite his weariness. "We've brought Emily back to her father. That's something to hold onto." His words were a balm to my troubled soul, offering comfort amid our shared sorrow. I nodded, trying to steady my breathing. Robert's presence was a grounding force, reminding me that while the night had brought its trials, we still had each other and the determination to keep moving forward.

The next morning, Robert and I settled into the quiet of the farmhouse, the night's events weighing heavily on us. After breakfast, Hill came in with Emily, who looked refreshed after her rest. She joined us at the table, where the dim light cast long shadows, and the air was thick with unanswered questions.

Emily looked up at us, her voice steady but tinged with fear. "I need to tell you everything," she said, gripping the edge of the table. "When I was taken, it was after I left college one evening. I was just walking back to my dorm when I was grabbed. I didn't see their faces; they blindfolded me immediately. I was moved to a different location—a building that seemed like an old hospital."

When she described the place, my heart sank. The description sounded eerily familiar. "An old hospital?" I echoed, trying to keep my voice calm. "Where exactly was this place?"

Emily shook her head. "I don't know. It was far from home. All I remember is that the building looked decrepit, with peeling paint and broken windows. It had a sterile smell, like old disinfectant."

Robert and I exchanged a look of realization. The description matched the old hospital we had visited earlier, the one where we had found the first clue about Emily. "You're talking about the same hospital we visited," Robert said, his voice low and thoughtful. "That's where we found the hint that led us to you."

Emily's eyes widened slightly. "Yes, that's the place. They kept me there for years. I have no idea why they kept me alive for so long."

Robert's brow furrowed. "That's the most surprising part. Why did they keep you alive all these years?"

Emily took a deep breath. "I know why. They believe my father has a secret code—something very important for their future operations. They think that if they keep me alive, my father will come to rescue me. They're using me as leverage, hoping to force him to reveal whatever secret code he has."

Robert turned to Hill, his expression serious. "Is this true? Do you have anything like that?"

Hill's face was a mask of confusion. "No, I don't

have anything like that. I'm not aware of any secret code."

Robert pressed further. "Think carefully. Is there anything you might have overlooked?"

Hill shook his head. "No, I don't remember anything like that."

Emily's voice was hesitant but insistent. "Maybe it's not with you. They often take the names of your associates or friends. I remember a name — Kevin."

"Kevin?" I leaned in, my pulse quickening. "Kevin Crater?"

She nodded. Robert's eyes widened. "Amanda, he's your stepbrother. I knew it. He's involved in all this."

Hill looked stunned. "Kevin Crater? Yes, I know him. He's my friend. We worked together at the same place. He was jobless and an orphan, just like me. That's why we ended up working for the same people."

The revelation hit me like a ton of bricks. Kevin, someone I had once known, had been orchestrating these heinous acts. The betrayal stung deeply, adding a layer of personal anguish to the already heavy burden of our mission. "I can't believe this," I said, my voice trembling. "Kevin caused so much harm to me and Clara."

Robert placed a reassuring hand on my shoulder. "It's a harsh truth, but it's one we need to face. Kevin's involvement changes everything. We need to be more cautious."

Emily's gaze was distant, her mind clearly processing the enormity of the situation. "We need to act fast. If they still think my father will come for me, they might be planning something even worse."

Robert nodded in agreement. We each took a moment to absorb the gravity of the situation. Emily's ordeal was over for now, but the fight was far from finished. Kevin's betrayal was a devastating blow, one that added urgency to our mission.

Despite her exhaustion, Emily tried to offer a small smile. "Thank you for saving me. I know there's still a lot to do, but I'm grateful to be out of there."

I returned her smile, though it was tinged with

sadness. "We'll get through this. We have to."

Robert's tone was resolute as he said, "Emily, rest now. We'll tackle everything."

Emily, with unwavering determination, replied, "No, I will go with you all. I can help you in a better way." Hill, after a moment's hesitation, nodded in agreement. "I'll stay with you too," he said. "We need to catch the real criminals, and I want to make sure that happens." His decision solidified the team's resolve as they prepared to face the daunting task ahead. We decided to leave for the hospital in two hours.

Afterward, I retreated from the living room to the small terrace outside. The cool night air felt like a balm against the emotional turmoil I was grappling with. The stars above seemed distant and indifferent, just as I felt. I leaned against the railing, my mind in disarray.

Robert followed me out, his presence a comforting weight against the coldness of the night. He approached quietly, his footsteps soft on the gravel. "Amanda," he said gently, placing a hand on my shoulder. "Be brave, please."

I turned to him, my eyes red and weary. "I feel like I am," I admitted, my voice breaking. "But everything is falling apart. I don't even know what to believe anymore."

Robert's gaze was warm and steady as he searched for the right words. "Sometimes, when everything seems dark, it's hard to see the way forward. But you don't have to face it alone."

I looked down, unable to meet his eyes. "It's not just the truth that's hurting me. It's the betrayal, the realization that Kevin, who I thought was innocent, might be involved in all of this."

He gently cupped my face in his hands, lifting my chin so that our eyes met. "Amanda, I know this is incredibly hard. But hiding from the truth won't make it go away. We need to face it together, no matter how painful it is."

I felt a tear slip down my cheek, and Robert wiped it away with his thumb. "I know you're strong enough to handle this," he said.

I took a deep breath, feeling the warmth of his hands on my face. "I don't know if I can. It feels like everything I believed in is crumbling."

Robert's voice was soothing, almost a whisper. "The truth will guide us to the answers we need and lead us to justice. We owe it to those who have suffered to see this through. And remember, I will be by your side always. I love you the most, and I will never leave you alone."

His words wrapped around me like a comforting embrace, and I found solace in his presence. "Thank you," I said softly, my voice steadying. "I needed to hear that." Robert pulled me into a gentle hug, his embrace strong and reassuring. "We'll get through this. I promise."

We stayed there for a while, wrapped in each other's arms, the air a quiet witness to our shared comfort. When we finally returned inside, we gathered around the table, spreading out documents and photographs as we planned our next move. The atmosphere was tense but focused. Emily was seated among us, her expression troubled.

As we examined the photographs, Emily's gaze fixed on one in particular. "Who is this girl?" she asked, pointing to a photograph of Clara.

I leaned in, my heart racing. "That's my sister, Clara. Do you know where she is?"

Emily's face fell, her voice trembling. "Yes, I've seen her before." Those words hit me like a sledgehammer. "Clara was kidnapped, and we are searching for her."

In shock, Emily replied, "What?! No, Clara isn't kidnapped. She's with the person who took me. I saw her with the crime master."

The revelation left me unsteady and disoriented. "That can't be true!" I yelled, my voice cracking. "Clara would never be involved in something like this. She's innocent!"

Emily's eyes filled with tears. "I know it's hard to believe, but it's the truth. I've told you everything I experienced."

Robert stepped in, his voice calm but firm. "Amanda, I know this is devastating. But we need to face the reality of the situation. We have to confront it to move forward." He took my hand, his touch warm and grounding. "It's not easy, Amanda. Accepting the truth is one of the hardest things to do, especially when it involves someone you love. But we have to. It's the only way to ensure that those responsible are held accountable."

I looked at Robert, his eyes filled with a mix of determination and compassion. "I don't know if I can handle this. It feels like my whole world is falling apart."

Robert squeezed my hand gently. "It's okay to feel that way. It's a heavy burden to bear. But staying true to the facts is crucial. It will bring us closer to justice and prevent more suffering. It's the right thing to do." His words resonated deeply within me, and I took a shuddering breath. "You're right. It's necessary. We need to uncover the truth, no matter how painful it is."

As we finalized our plans to investigate the hospital further, my phone rang. It was my neighbor, her voice tinged with urgency. "Amanda, there are large parcels outside your house. You need to come back immediately.

Fear gripped me. What could this mean? We

hastily packed up and drove back to my home, the car ride filled with anxious silence. When we arrived, my neighbor pointed to the front porch, where several large parcels were stacked haphazardly. My heart pounded as we opened them.

Inside, we found documents, photographs, and various items all centered on Clara. The contents were damning, portraying her as a criminal working alongside Miss Olivia. There was also a tape recording and several notes from an unknown sender.

My hands trembled as I unwrapped the tape and notes. I played the recording on my phone, tears welling up in my eyes. Clara's voice echoed through the room, speaking with Miss Olivia. The conversation was chilling, seemingly confirming her involvement in illegal activities. My heart ached, unable to reconcile this with the sister I knew and loved.

The notes were even more unsettling, containing threats and warnings: "We said not to explore or you'd be in danger. This time, you are hurt more." It was clear someone was trying to manipulate us, to sow distrust and fear.

"This can't be true," I whispered, my voice breaking. "Clara would never be involved in something like this. There has to be another explanation."

Robert approached me, his expression a mix of empathy and resolve. "Amanda, I understand how hard this is. It's a blow to everything you believed in. But we need to confront these facts, no matter how painful they are."

Tears streamed down my cheeks. "I can't believe it. I won't accept it. Clara has always been kind and caring. This recording must be a fabrication." Robert put a comforting arm around me. "We need to face it head-on to uncover the full picture. It's the only way to bring justice and find out what really happened."

I looked at him with desperate eyes. "But why? Why would they do this? What if Clara is really guilty? I don't want to believe it."

Robert held my gaze, his expression serious. "No one is going to believe anything until we find Clara. I have experience as a detective, and I know that just because something looks true doesn't mean it is. This could be a manipulation by the real criminals to divert us from discovering the truth. We need to stay calm and continue our investigation. We can't make any decisions or accusations until we have all the facts."

Hill added, "Yes, someone might have created this evidence to frame Clara, to make it seem like she's involved when she's not. But the only way to find out is to keep digging, to follow every lead, no matter how difficult it might be."

With heavy hearts, we gathered the evidence and prepared to return to the hospital. The truth was elusive and painful, but we had no choice but to pursue it.

Chapter 8

The Handwriting of Betrayal

Robert's gaze was intense as he scanned the notes spread out on the table before him. "We need to know who's sending these notes," he declared firmly, his voice filled with a certainty that left no room for argument.

Hill stepped forward, taking the notes from my hands. His experienced eyes scrutinized each one with meticulous care. After a few minutes of silence, he suddenly looked up, recognition etched on his face. "Wait, I recognize this handwriting. It's Kevin's. I'm certain about it. We worked together extensively."

Robert's jaw tightened. "So, Kevin is involved in this after all," he said, frustration and resolve lacing his tone. "I have a plan to expose him. Hill, call Kevin and ask him to meet us. We need to confront him directly."

Hill nodded and made the call. Within minutes, Kevin agreed to meet us at a nearby park the next morning. The park was quiet and secluded—perfect for a discreet conversation. When we arrived, we stationed ourselves strategically, ready to catch Kevin in the act of deception.

Kevin arrived punctually, his demeanor slightly uneasy. Hill approached him first. "Kevin, thanks for coming," he said, keeping his tone neutral but firm.

"What's this about?" Kevin asked, glancing around with evident discomfort.

Robert stepped forward, his presence commanding. "Kevin, we need to talk about these notes you've been sending to Amanda."

Kevin's eyes widened in feigned innocence. "I don't know what you're talking about."

Hill held up one of the notes. "Don't play dumb, Kevin. I recognize your handwriting. We worked together for years."

Kevin's eyes darted around, his frustration evident. "That's not my handwriting, Hill! You've got the wrong guy."

Hill remained unfazed, his gaze steely. "I'm not letting you squirm out of this. You always put a line and an asterisk at the end of your notes. It's your signature, and look, each note has it, Kevin."

Kevin's defiance wavered as Hill continued. "And remember that letter you kept in your pocket? The one you wrote for your mother who passed away? You once told me you believed that one day you'd meet her again and tell her how much you missed her. You even showed me part of it—the letter was meant to convey how deeply you felt her absence."

Robert checked his pocket and pulled out a letter. After matching the two handwritings, it was clear: Kevin was the one sending the notes.

Realization dawned on Kevin's face, and he sighed, looking defeated. "Alright, I sent the notes. But I didn't mean for things to get out of hand."

I stepped forward. "Kevin, why?" My voice trembled, not with fear but with the weight of betrayal. "How could you do this to me and to us?"

Kevin met my gaze, and for a moment, the park

fell silent. "Amanda, I... I thought you both were involved in Mom's death. I was blinded by my grief and anger."

My eyes narrowed, tears forming but refusing to fall. "We were family, Kevin. You chose to torment me instead of seeking the truth. Do you know what that did to me? I lost Clara."

Kevin looked away, shame flooding his features. "I never wanted it to go this far. I just... I just wanted answers."

I stepped closer, my voice now a whisper, laced with years of pain. "You tore me apart, Kevin. We didn't take your mother's life. You don't even know what I did to save her. I gave all my savings to the doctor for her operation, but she came with a short life expectancy. Wait, let me clear this up for you." I pulled out my phone and called the doctor. When she answered, I asked her to explain everything to Kevin.

After listening to the doctor's words, Kevin's face crumpled, shame and regret washing over him. "I'm so sorry, Amanda," he whispered, tears streaming down his face. "I'll do everything I can to make it right.

Please forgive me for all the wrong I've done."

Robert's gaze was stern. "Do you realize the danger you've put Amanda in with your actions? And what about the recordings? Are they fake too?"

Kevin nodded, a pained look on his face. "Yes, the recordings are fake. I used software to manipulate the audio. I wanted Amanda to feel scared and confused, just like I've felt all these years."

Robert's expression softened slightly, but his tone remained serious. "Kevin, this isn't just a family feud anymore. Your actions have real consequences, and we need to focus on finding Clara and dealing with the actual criminals."

Kevin looked down, visibly remorseful. "I'm sorry. I didn't think it would go this far. I just wanted some kind of retribution."

Hill placed a supportive hand on Kevin's shoulder. "Kevin, we all have our struggles, but this isn't the way to handle them. We need to unite to find the real criminals and save Clara."

Kevin nodded, his eyes brimming with tears. "I understand. I'll stop interfering. I'll help however I can."

We left the park with a renewed sense of clarity and purpose. Kevin's involvement had been a personal vendetta rather than a direct link to the criminal network. We needed to refocus on the larger picture: finding Clara and dismantling the organization responsible for the crimes.

Back at our base, Robert laid out the next steps. "We need to revisit the hospital. If the criminals are using it as a base, we need to gather concrete evidence."

Hill agreed, adding, "Emily mentioned a building behind the hospital where illegal activities take place. That's where we should direct our search."

The following day, we prepared for action. Armed with cameras, recording devices, and other investigative tools, we approached the hospital with a mix of anticipation and apprehension. The structure loomed over us, its decaying façade hiding dark secrets.

Inside, we navigated the dark hallways with caution, guided by Emily's detailed description of the layout. We reached the rear of the building, where Emily had indicated the hidden area.

Our search was methodical. We split up, each of us examining different rooms and documenting our findings. It quickly became apparent that the building had been used for various illicit activities. We uncovered evidence of medical experiments, financial records, and other incriminating materials.

In a dimly lit office at the back of the building, Robert and I regrouped. "We have enough evidence to take action," he said, his tone resolute. "But we still need to find Clara."

As we prepared to leave, we heard footsteps approaching. We quickly hid, waiting to see who it was. Two men entered the room, discussing plans for a new operation. Their conversation revealed their involvement in the criminal network.

We recorded their dialogue, capturing crucial details that could lead us to Clara. Once they departed, we made our way out of the hospital, eager to review the evidence we had gathered.

Back at our base, we pieced together the clues.

It was evident that we were closing in on Clara's location. The evidence from the hospital was pivotal, but we had to remain vigilant. The criminals we were up against were dangerous, and any misstep could jeopardize our mission.

Robert turned to me, his eyes filled with determination. "We're going to find Clara. We're going to bring her home and ensure these criminals face justice." I nodded, feeling a renewed sense of hope. With Robert by my side, I knew we had a fighting chance to uncover the truth and rescue Clara from those who had taken her.

Chapter 9

Clara's Revelation

As we neared Clara, I sensed her location thanks to a pendant our mother had given us—a unique family heirloom. The pendant was divided into two halves: one piece with me and the other around Clara's neck. This pendant was special; when the two halves were brought together, they emitted a blue light. It was said that if either half came near a similar stone, it would begin to blink, guiding us to its location.

Following this lead, we discovered that Clara's pendant was now near the same building behind the hospital we had visited before. The area was marked by a solitary oak tree, and beside this tree was an unassuming room in the building—a room that had seen better days.

With the location clearly defined, Robert and I decided to proceed into the building. The fading daylight cast long shadows around the dilapidated structure, and the solitary oak tree stood as a silent witness to our next move. The crumbling walls and broken windows hinted at years of neglect, but we couldn't afford to hesitate.

"Let's go," I said, my voice firm despite the creeping unease. Robert nodded in agreement, his expression resolute. He instructed Hill and Emily to stay outside. "Keep an eye on the surroundings and let us know if anything seems off."

Hill gave a terse nod, his eyes scanning the area with a mixture of vigilance and concern. Emily, standing close beside him, appeared anxious but understanding. She clutched Hill's arm tightly, drawing comfort from his presence as they took their positions near the entrance.

Robert and I approached the entrance, our hearts pounding with anticipation and dread. As we stepped inside the dimly lit room, our eyes fell on Clara. She was barely recognizable; her eyes, once bright and full of life, were now dull and hollow, and her body frail and weakened. She lay on a cot, a stark contrast to the vibrant person I remembered.

I knelt beside Clara, my heart pounding in my chest. "Clara, my sister," I whispered, my voice trembling with emotion. "It's me, Amanda. We found you."

Clara's eyes flickered with recognition, her face a mixture of relief and disbelief. She reached out a trembling hand, her voice barely audible. "Finally, Amanda... you came."

Tears welled up in my eyes, spilling over as I took her hand in mine, holding it tightly. "I never stopped looking for you," I said, my voice choked with emotion. "Not for a single moment."

Clara's grip tightened, and a faint smile played on her lips. "I knew... I knew you'd come. I never gave up hope."

Robert knelt beside us, his hand gently resting on Clara's shoulder. "You're safe now, Clara," he said. "We'll make sure of it."

Clara looked between us, her eyes brimming

with tears. "I was so scared... so alone. But I held on because I knew you wouldn't give up on me."

With a gentle voice, Robert said, "Let's go from here. We don't have time, and we can't afford to take any risks now." Soon, we all managed to escape from the building, moving swiftly and silently through the shadows until we reached a safe place near the hospital. Once inside, we locked the door and breathed a collective sigh of relief.

Clara sat down, her body visibly relaxing. "I can't believe it's over," she whispered, tears of relief streaming down her face. "Thank you... all of you."

I sat beside her, wrapping my arm around her shoulders. "It's over now, Clara. You're safe, and we're here. I won't let anything happen to you."

Robert nodded, standing guard by the door. "We'll stay here until it's safe to move again. Rest now, Clara." Clara leaned against me, closing her eyes. For the first time in what felt like an eternity, she allowed herself to relax, knowing she was finally free from her nightmare.

The next morning, the first rays of sunlight

filtered through the curtains, casting a soft glow across the room. Clara stirred beside me, her eyes fluttering open. For a moment, she looked disoriented, but then relief washed over her face as she remembered she was safe.

"Good morning," I whispered, brushing a strand of hair from her face. "How are you feeling?"

Clara smiled weakly. "Better. A bit sore, but... better."

Robert walked over with a tray of breakfast he had managed to prepare. "I thought you might be hungry," he said, placing the tray on the table. "Eat something. It'll help you regain your strength."

Clara nodded, reaching for a piece of toast. "Thank you," she said softly, her voice filled with gratitude. "Both of you. I don't know what I would have done without you."

I squeezed her hand reassuringly. "You don't have to worry about that now. We're together, and we'll face whatever comes next together.

Then Robert asked, "Clara, can you tell us what happened exactly? We need to know everything."

Clara took a deep breath, her voice shaking as she began to speak. "It all started with Miss Olivia. She trapped me with her manipulative ways. I thought she needed my help. She told me she was in danger and that I had to keep it a secret, even from you, Amanda. She knew I loved her and saw her as a mother figure. I agreed to help her, thinking I was doing the right thing."

She paused, her eyes glazing over with the memory. "One day, just before my disappearance, I went to meet Miss Olivia. I found her in a meeting with some very dangerous people. They were discussing operations that sounded sinister. My presence shocked Miss Olivia; she thought I had overheard their plans. But I was clueless. She manipulated me into thinking she was in grave danger and needed my help. She swore me to secrecy, forcing me to promise not to tell anyone, especially not you, Amanda."

Clara's grip on my hand tightened as she continued. "I mostly went there to help her after that. I was so naive. I believed her lies because I trusted her so much. She had always been so kind to me. But that day after the festival, everything changed. I went to see Miss Olivia, and she took me to an old, decrepit hospital. Inside, there were patients in terrible condition. She told me they were laborers being operated on for free, but they were actually victims of illegal medical experiments. They had no records, no identities. If they died, they would be hidden forever."

A shiver ran down my spine as Clara's words sank in. The pieces of the puzzle were finally coming together, but the picture they formed was horrifying.

"Clara," Robert said softly, "why did Miss Olivia involve you in this?"

"She made me believe that if I didn't help, those people would suffer even more," Clara replied, tears streaming down her face. "I thought I was saving lives. But in reality, I was being used to cover up their crimes. Miss Olivia was part of a larger operation, and she needed someone she could manipulate and control. She knew I wouldn't refuse her."

I felt a surge of anger and sadness. Miss Olivia, whom I had trusted and admired, had betrayed us in the worst possible way. "Why didn't you tell me,

Clara? I could have helped."

Clara shook her head, her eyes wide with fear. "I was terrified, Amanda. Miss Olivia made it clear that if I told anyone, especially you, it would be disastrous. She said that if this information got out, it would endanger all our patients because there's someone who wants to see them harmed. I didn't know what to do. I thought I was protecting them."

Robert nodded, understanding the gravity of Clara's predicament. "Clara, we need to know more about these operations. What exactly were they doing in that hospital? We have a lot of evidence against the criminals now, but we need to know everything from you. Maybe we're missing something."

Clara's voice trembled as she recounted the details. "They were performing illegal surgeries, experimenting on people without their consent. Most of the patients were laborers who had been promised free medical care. But instead, they were subjected to horrific procedures. Some of them didn't survive. Miss Olivia and her associates would dispose of the bodies to avoid leaving any evidence. It was a nightmare,

Amanda. I wanted to escape, but I didn't know how."

The weight of Clara's revelation hung heavily in the room. The scope of Miss Olivia's deception was staggering, and the implications were even more chilling. We had to act quickly to bring these criminals to justice and stop their crimes.

"We're going to expose them," Robert said firmly. Clara nodded weakly. "I'll do whatever I can. I don't want anyone else to suffer because of them."

I felt a glimmer of hope. We were one step closer to justice, and with Clara by our side, we knew we had the strength to see it through to the end.

Chapter 10

The Dark Truth Unveiled

Then, the tension in the room grew palpable as Emily spoke out. "You're lying," Emily said, her voice trembling with a mix of anger and confusion. "When I was kidnapped, you were with them. You weren't there forcefully. I remember clearly seeing you with all of them many times."

Clara took a deep breath, her face etched with a mixture of guilt and determination. "Emily, you have to understand that, at that time, I didn't know what they were truly involved in. I was there to help Miss Olivia. She told me you were just a patient's daughter, and after he died, you had a breakdown. She made it sound like it was all a misunderstanding."

Emily shook her head, tears welling up in her

eyes. "But you looked so... complicit."

Clara's eyes filled with sorrow as she continued. "I know it seemed that way, but I was just as deceived as everyone else. Miss Olivia manipulated me and played on my emotions. I looked up to her like a mother. When she told me you were in distress, I believed her."

Robert, standing beside Emily, put a comforting hand on her shoulder. "Let's hear her out, Emily," he urged gently.

Clara nodded gratefully at Robert before continuing. "When I finally discovered the truth about Miss Olivia's operations, I was horrified. I knew I had to do something, so I started secretly collecting evidence against her. I documented everything I could without raising suspicion."

"Why didn't you come to us for help?" Emily asked, her voice softer now but still tinged with pain.

Clara explained, "By the time I realized what was happening, it was too late. Miss Olivia had me under constant watch. She knew I was getting suspicious. When I refused to hand over the evidence, she kidnapped me and tortured me, trying to break me. But I never gave in. I kept the evidence hidden, hoping for a chance to expose her."

A silence fell over the room as we absorbed Clara's words. The weight of her courage and resilience was evident. She had risked everything to bring justice to the victims of Miss Olivia's heinous crimes.

"Where is the evidence now?" Robert asked, his detective instincts kicking in.

Clara took a deep breath. "I hid it in a safe place, away from her reach. I can take you there."

Robert nodded, his expression resolute. "We'll go together. It's time to end this once and for all."

Emily, still visibly shaken, stepped closer to Clara. "I'm sorry for doubting you," she said, her voice barely above a whisper. "I didn't understand."

Clara reached out and took Emily's hand. "You had every right to question me. But now, we need to work together to make sure Miss Olivia and her husband face justice."

As we prepared to retrieve the hidden evidence,

I couldn't help but feel a renewed sense of purpose. Clara's bravery had given us the final piece of the puzzle. We were close to bringing down the entire operation and freeing the victims from their torment.

We set out that evening, following Clara's lead to the location where she had hidden the evidence. It was a small, dilapidated shed on the outskirts of town—a place no one would think to look. Clara led us inside and carefully lifted a loose floorboard, revealing a metal box. She opened it to reveal a trove of documents, photographs, and recordings. The evidence was irrefutable.

The room fell silent as Clara laid out the damning evidence on the table. Photographs of clandestine surgeries, forged medical records, and financial transactions traced back to offshore accounts all pointed to Miss Olivia and her husband's involvement in illegal activities.

"These pieces of evidence," Clara began, her voice cutting through the tension, "alongside the evidence you already possess, will lead to a conviction for illegal surgeries. They'll get a sentence that's a fraction of what they truly deserve. The real crime, however, is far more sinister. Olivia and her husband are deeply entrenched in serious crime—a clandestine operation that has remained hidden from the authorities."

Clara had more to reveal. "There's more you need to know about Miss Olivia," she began, her voice steady despite the gravity of her words. "She and her husband were not just involved in illegal surgeries. They were part of a much darker operation."

Robert leaned forward, his expression serious. "Go on, Clara."

Clara took a deep breath. "Miss Olivia and her husband would travel to faraway villages—places where people were desperate for work and medical help. They would promise these poor laborers jobs and free medical care. But once they had them under their control, they would deceive them and perform surgeries without their consent."

The room grew colder as Clara continued, the horror of her words sinking in. "They were involved in organ trafficking. They would harvest organs from these unsuspecting laborers and sell them through illicit trade. The people who survived the surgeries were left in terrible conditions, with no idea what had been done to them. Those who didn't survive were disposed of, their bodies hidden to avoid detection."

Robert's jaw tightened, and his fists clenched on the table. "But we found many pieces of evidence confirming they were working as a group involved in break-ins, bribery, and more."

Clara nodded, her eyes reflecting the gravity of the situation. "Yes, that was just the beginning," she continued. "They had partnerships with some groups involved in these activities, but soon they departed from those missions. Over time, their greed grew, and they transitioned into something far more sinister — organ trafficking. They would harvest organs from unsuspecting laborers and sell them on the black market."

"How did you find out about this, Clara?" Robert asked, his voice low and intense.

Clara's eyes filled with tears. "I stumbled upon it by accident. One day, I saw Miss Olivia and her husband bringing in a group of laborers. They looked so hopeful, believing they were finally getting the help they needed. But later, I overheard a conversation between Miss Olivia and her husband. They were discussing organ sales and planning their next move. I was horrified. I didn't know what to do."

Robert nodded, his expression grim. "We need to gather as much evidence as we can. This has to stop."

I reached out and took Clara's hand. "Clara, you're incredibly brave, and we're going to make sure they pay for what they've done." Clara squeezed my hand.

"I couldn't live with myself if I didn't do something to stop them. They need to be brought to justice."

A gasp escaped my lips. The sheer cruelty and ruthlessness of Miss Olivia's actions were beyond anything I could have imagined.

Clara took a deep breath, the weight of her next revelation heavy on her shoulders. "There's more," she said, her voice dropping to a near whisper. "Miss Olivia's orphanage isn't a place of refuge or charity. It's a front for her real business. She raises those innocent children only to sell their organs later. By sheer luck, a few might escape, but for most, it's a death sentence."

The room gasped in horror, the full extent of Olivia's depravity sinking in. Clara continued, looking directly at me, "You and I were fortunate. We escaped because, at the time, Olivia was preoccupied with her husband's new hospital renovation. She didn't focus on keeping us locked inside. We were so close to becoming her next victims, but God saved us. I believe we are meant to save others, and that's why."

"We can't let more children suffer the same fate. We need to expose her entire operation — not just the illegal surgeries, but the organ trafficking as well. This is bigger than we thought, and we have to act fast."

Robert, regaining his composure, leaned forward. "What's our next move? Clara, do you have anything in mind or any plan that can expose Olivia's real crimes?"

Clara took a deep breath, her eyes filled with determination. "Yes, I do. We need to go undercover and catch them in the act."

She laid out her strategy, her voice unwavering. "We'll disguise ourselves as laborers seeking medical help. Only Robert and Emily will stay outside, coordinating everything. The rest of us will go inside with hidden cameras and recorders that transmit live footage back to Robert and Emily. We'll wait for the operation to start, and then we'll broadcast everything live on every TV and radio channel worldwide, exposing their crimes openly."

Robert nodded, impressed by the bold plan. "That's risky, but it could work. We need to make sure our disguises are perfect and our equipment is flawless."

At the same time, Emily raised a crucial concern. "We need an expert to manage the broadcast. We can't afford any risks; one slip-up, and we're all trapped. But the point is, we can't hire anyone we don't know because Miss Olivia has many connections. If someone decides to betray us at the last moment, it could be disastrous."

Robert nodded thoughtfully. "So, who do we trust with this? We need someone reliable and skilled."

Hill, who had been quietly listening, spoke up. "I know one person who can handle this perfectly, but he might not be willing to help us."

Robert turned to him, curiosity piqued. "Who is it? Tell us more."

Hill hesitated before answering, "His name is Kevin. He's an old friend and an expert in this kind of work. But there's a catch. Kevin has a troubled past and might be hesitant to get involved."

Clara's expression darkened. "Kevin? Are you serious? He was involved in criminal activities. How can we trust him? I can't believe you'd even suggest him."

Hill sighed, understanding her concern. "I know what you're thinking, Clara. But Kevin has changed. He's been trying to make amends. Besides, we don't have many options. He's the best we have for this job."

Clara shook her head, frustration evident. "I can't trust him. He's my brother, and I know what he's done. I've had my own share of bad experiences, and I can't risk everything on him. I can't even think of harming anyone, but Kevin... he has a dark past."

Robert, trying to mediate, suggested, "Let's hear him out. Maybe he's genuinely changed. We'll be careful and ensure everything is in place to prevent any betrayal."

As they debated, the doorbell rang. Robert walked over to open the door, and there stood Kevin.

Kevin looked hesitant but determined. "I heard you need my help," he began, looking directly at Clara. "I know I've done terrible things in the past, and I'm truly sorry. I've been trying to change and make up for my mistakes. I want to help you bring Olivia down."

Clara's eyes narrowed, skepticism clear in her expression. "Why should we believe you? How do we know you won't betray us?"

Kevin took a deep breath. "I was embarrassed about what I had done, so I chased you all and wanted to join you. I'm not someone who can take a life. When I realized what was happening, I was disturbed and shocked. That's why I cut myself off from everything. I understand that losing someone you love is the biggest pain. I still want my mother. I can't forget her. Please give me one chance to help you."

I stepped forward and said, "Okay, we will."

Robert, still cautious, interjected, "We can't trust him blindly."

Clara echoed the sentiment. "How can we?"

I turned to them and insisted, "We have to trust him now. We have no option left. And as far as I know, Kevin has never lied about his mother's name. I trust him."

The room fell silent as everyone processed my words. Clara finally nodded, albeit reluctantly. "Alright, Kevin. You get one chance. But if you do anything to jeopardize this operation, I won't hesitate to stop you myself."

Kevin nodded, understanding the gravity of the situation. "Thank you. I won't let you down."

The whole team spent the next few days preparing meticulously. They acquired labor outfits, disguised their appearances, and tested the hidden cameras and recorders.

Kevin contacted a trusted journalist friend who agreed to help ensure that the live broadcast reached as many people as possible.

On the day of the operation, the team split up. Clara and a few others entered the hospital in their disguises, blending in seamlessly. Robert and Kevin stayed outside in a van, monitoring the live feeds from the hidden cameras.

Inside the hospital, Clara and her team mingled with the real laborers, acting as though they were seeking medical help. They managed to get themselves selected for the next round of "treatments." As they were led into the operating rooms, the hidden cameras captured everything, transmitting live footage back to Robert and Kevin.

Robert, watching the screens intently, turned to Kevin. "It's time. Are you ready?"

Kevin nodded, his finger hovering over the button that would send the live feed to every TV and radio station. "Ready."

As the operation began, Miss Olivia and her husband entered the room, discussing their next move openly, believing they were safe within the confines of their hospital. The cameras captured their every word.

"These organs will fetch a good price," Miss

Olivia said with a cold smile. "Make sure to dispose of the bodies properly this time."

Clara, with a hidden microphone, whispered into her transmitter, "Now, Kevin. Do it now."

Kevin pressed the button, and the live feed was broadcast worldwide. TV screens and radios across the globe suddenly filled with horrifying scenes from the hospital. People watched in shock as the true nature of Miss Olivia's operations was revealed.

Inside the hospital, chaos erupted as the staff realized they had been exposed. Police, tipped off by Robert, stormed the building, arresting Miss Olivia, her husband, and their accomplices.

The journalist, watching the events unfold from a safe distance, provided live commentary, ensuring that the world understood the full extent of the crimes committed.

As Miss Olivia and her husband were led away in handcuffs, their faces twisted in anger and disbelief, Clara and her team emerged from the hospital, exhausted but victorious.

Clara ran up to me and hugged me tightly. "We

did it! The whole world knows about us."

Robert joined us, pride evident in his eyes. "Your plan was brilliant, Clara. You brought them down."

Clara smiled, though the weight of the ordeal was clear in her expression. "We did it together. Now, we can start helping the victims rebuild their lives."

As we stood there, watching the news coverage of the arrests, a sense of collective relief and accomplishment washed over us. The magnitude of what we had achieved settled in, and for a moment, the gravity of our actions silenced us. Together, we had exposed a monstrous operation, bringing justice to those who had suffered in silence for far too long.

Chapter 11

A New Dawn

The air was thick with the anticipation of a new beginning. The nightmare that had plagued our lives for so long was finally over. Miss Olivia and her husband were behind bars, and their organ trafficking ring had been dismantled. Justice was being served, and the victims were receiving the care they needed.

Together, as a strong team, we stood in the hospital courtyard, watching the sunrise. The first light of dawn symbolized the end of our darkness and the start of a brighter future.

"Thank you all," Clara said, breaking the serene silence. "I couldn't have done this without you."

I squeezed her hand. "We did it together, Clara. Your bravery and determination led us here."

Robert nodded, his usually stern face softened by a rare smile. "We make a good team. But this isn't the end. We have to make sure this never happens again."

Emily, who had been quiet, finally spoke up. "We need to help the victims. They deserve a chance at a normal life."

Kevin, standing beside Emily, nodded in agreement. "We should also raise awareness to prevent this from happening to anyone else."

Hill added, "Education and support are crucial. We need to create a safe space for these victims to rebuild their lives."

We all agreed, and over the next few weeks, we worked tirelessly to support the victims. Clara used her knowledge of the operation to help authorities locate hidden safe houses and rescue more people. Emily and I volunteered at shelters, offering our time and resources wherever needed. Meanwhile, Kevin and Hill organized community outreach programs and educational workshops.

One evening, as we gathered around the dinner

table, Emily looked at Clara, her eyes a mix of admiration and sorrow. "I'm so sorry for everything you went through. I wish I had known sooner."

Clara offered a gentle smile. "You have nothing to apologize for, Emily. We're here now, and that's what matters."

Watching them, I felt a deep sense of pride. Our journey had been filled with pain and uncertainty, but it had also brought us closer. The bond between us was unbreakable.

Robert cleared his throat, catching our attention. "I have an idea," he said, a spark of inspiration in his eyes. "Why don't we start a foundation? We could use our experiences to help others, prevent these kinds of horrors, and support the survivors."

The room fell silent as we took in his suggestion. It was a brilliant idea—one that could turn our suffering into something good, a lasting legacy.

"That's a wonderful idea," I said, feeling a surge of excitement. "We could name it after our journey. Something that symbolizes hope and resilience."

"How about The Dawn Foundation?" Clara

suggested. "It represents a new beginning, just like the dawn of a new day."

We all nodded in agreement. It was perfect.

Over the next several months, we worked tirelessly to establish The Dawn Foundation. Partnering with local and international organizations, we raised awareness about human trafficking and provided resources for victims. Our efforts were met with overwhelming support from the community.

One sunny afternoon, we held our first official event. The turnout was incredible, with people from all walks of life gathered to support our cause. Standing on stage, we looked out at the sea of faces, united by hope and purpose, and felt a profound sense of gratitude and accomplishment. This was just the beginning of something truly meaningful.

Clara stepped forward, her voice steady and confident. "Thank you all for being here today. The Dawn Foundation was born out of darkness, but it stands for hope and a brighter future. Together, we can make a difference."

The crowd erupted in applause, filling me with

pride. This was our legacy—a testament to our strength and unity. Later, I found a quiet moment to stand beside Robert. "We did it," I said, my voice thick with emotion.

He nodded, his eyes mirroring the pride and relief I felt. "Yes, we did. And this is just the beginning."

That evening, we returned to the hospital courtyard, where our journey had come full circle. The sunset painted the sky in hues of orange and pink—a striking contrast to the dark times we had overcome.

We stood together, watching the sun dip below the horizon. The future was uncertain, but we faced it with unwavering resolve.

"We've come so far," Clara said softly. "And there's still so much to do."

I smiled, feeling deeply fulfilled. "We'll do it together—as a family."

Emily took Kevin's hand, embracing a new beginning as they found comfort and strength in each other. Robert placed a reassuring hand on my shoulder, and I leaned into him, grateful for the love and support we shared.

As stars began to twinkle in the night sky, we made a silent promise: to keep fighting for justice, to protect the innocent, and to honor the journey that had brought us here.

The Dawn Foundation thrived, becoming a beacon of hope for many. Our story was one of resilience, courage, and the unbreakable bond of family. Moving forward, we carried the light of dawn with us, illuminating the path to a better future.

Months passed quickly, filled with hard work and the joy of new beginnings. Robert and I grew closer, our bond deepening with each passing day. One warm afternoon, Robert surprised me in the very courtyard where our journey had turned a corner.

"Amanda," he began, taking my hands in his, "we've been through so much together, and I can't wait any longer. Will you marry me?"

Tears of joy filled my eyes as I nodded. "Yes, Robert. I will."

Our wedding was held in the very courtyard where we faced our darkest moments. It wasn't just a union of two people; it was a celebration of the strength we had found in each other and the journey we had undertaken together. The ceremony was beautiful and intimate, surrounded by our closest family and friends. Clara, Emily, Kevin, and Hill stood by our side, their support a testament to the bonds we had forged through our shared trials. As we exchanged our vows, I felt an overwhelming sense of peace and joy, knowing we were beginning a new chapter together.

Not long after our wedding, Kevin and Emily announced their engagement. The joy in their eyes was evident as Kevin slipped a ring onto Emily's finger during a small gathering at our home.

"Emily," Kevin said softly, "you've brought light into my life, and I want to spend the rest of my days with you. Will you marry me?" Emily's eyes sparkled with tears of happiness as she replied, "Yes, Kevin. I can't wait to spend my life with you."

The engagement celebration was filled with laughter, love, and the warmth of friends who had become family. We toasted to new beginnings and the bright future ahead.

Our journey had been filled with trials, but it had also led us to a place of hope and happiness. With the strength of our bonds and the promise of new adventures, we faced the future with unwavering resolve, knowing that together we could overcome anything. The light of dawn had brought us to this moment, and we were ready to embrace whatever lay ahead, hand in hand.

Epilogue

A year later,

As I stand on the balcony of our apartment in Silver Creek, watching the town awaken in the early morning light, I'm struck by how far we've come. The transition from the darkness of our past to the vibrant, hopeful present feels almost surreal.

It has been a year since we founded The Dawn Foundation, and while the transformation has been remarkable, what truly stands out is how our lives have evolved. Clara, now a respected leader in global awareness campaigns, has discovered a new rhythm in her life. Her work continues to make a difference, but it's her personal growth and newfound balance that bring her the most joy. She's engaged to a wonderful partner who shares her passion for social causes, and together they are building a life filled with love and purpose.

Emily and Kevin, now happily married, have embraced their roles within the community with unwavering dedication. Their new home has become a hub of warmth and hospitality, where friends and family gather regularly. They are expecting their first child, and their excitement is palpable. Their journey together is a testament to love and perseverance, shaping their lives and the lives of those around them.

Robert and I have found our rhythm as well. As the executive director of The Dawn Foundation, I'm dedicated to advancing our mission, but it's our quiet moments together that mean the most. Robert's return from abroad brought him back to his roots, and he's now involved in local initiatives aligned with his passion for community service. His mother's recovery allowed him to reconnect with his dreams, and he's found fulfillment in both his professional and personal lives.

This year's Harvest Festival brought the

community together in a joyous celebration of autumn. The festival was filled with laughter, music, and the warmth of shared experiences. The streets of Silver Creek were adorned with vibrant decorations, and the air was rich with the aroma of freshly baked pies and roasted chestnuts. The festival reminded us of the beauty of our small town and the strength of its people.

As Robert and I walked hand in hand through the festival, surrounded by the sights and sounds of our community, I felt a profound sense of peace. We stopped at a booth where Clara and her fiancé were volunteering; their smiles reflected their contentment. Emily and Kevin soon joined us, their excitement about the future evident in every conversation.

Standing together, we reflected on our journey and the transformations that had shaped our lives. Robert squeezed my hand, his eyes filled with warmth. "It's incredible to think about how much has changed."

I nodded, feeling the weight of our shared history. "It does feel like a different world, but it's been an amazing journey." Robert's gaze drifted over the festival. "I'm proud of everything we've achieved. We've made a real difference."

I leaned closer and said, "Me too. And we'll keep making a difference—together."

As the sun set over Silver Creek, casting a golden hue over the festival, I knew our journey was far from over. With each new day, we face the future with hope and determination, ready to embrace whatever lies ahead. Our lives are intertwined with those we love, and together, we continue to illuminate the path forward.

About the Author

Bushra Hafeez, a passionate thriller enthusiast, invites you to embark on a gripping journey through storytelling seen from the eyes of suspects. Her debut novel, The Vanishing Point, masterfully blends imagination and reality, filled with intriguing "what ifs" and "buts," promising an unforgettable adventure of twists and turns.

This thriller is designed to keep you on the edge of your seat, featuring strong, character-driven plots where past events lead to present consequences. With fast-paced situations and lives hanging in the balance, each page holds a secret waiting to be uncovered.

Growing up amidst the vibrant, diverse cultures of New York, Bushra's keen interest in observing and analyzing human behavior—coupled with a minor in psychology—fuels her exploration of complex characters and intricate plots. So, take a seat and prepare to be drawn into her captivating story!

Note from the Author

Dear Reader,

Thank you *for choosing to read my book! I hope you enjoyed the journey as much as I enjoyed writing it. Your feedback is invaluable to me. If you have a moment, please consider leaving a review to share your thoughts and help other readers discover this story.*

I'd love to keep in touch and share more with you! If you'd like to be the first to hear about new releases, exclusive content, and special giveaways, please consider joining my newsletter at www.bushrahafeezveilpress.com .
Thank you for your support!